THE WOMAN WHO

THE WOMAN WHO
LOVED CUCUMBERS

Contemporary short stories by women from Wales

Edited by

PATRICIA DUNCKER & JANET THOMAS

HONNO MODERN FICTION

Published by Honno
'Ailsa Craig', Heol y Cawl, Dinas Powys,
South Glamorgan, Wales, CF6 4AH.

British Library Cataloguing in Publication Data

The Woman who Loved Cucumbers
1. Title

ISBN 1 870206 49 5

Published with the financial support of the
Arts Council of Wales

Acknowledgements:
'The Woman who loved cucumbers'
was first published in
Everywoman Magazine (London 1994).

Cover design by Debbie Maidment

Photograph of Elvis with kind permission of
Elvis Presley Enterprises Inc.

Typeset and printed in Wales by Gwasg Dinefwr, Llandybïe

CONTENTS

FOREWORD

Food has always been a powerful theme in fiction. It brings together so many different areas of our lives – families, celebration, ceremonies, survival. Everyone has a story about food. Our only worry was that they'd all be the same – cosy, nostalgic family rituals. But when the submissions came in, it soon became clear that if you ask women to discuss food, comfort is not the over-riding emotion.

Food is a dangerous territory. We had stories of poisoning, of women imprisoned in caring for others. Stories of bullying, bribery and suicidal self-denial. By far the most frequent topic was body image. Food equalling weight. Not positive images, but again and again, fat equalling obesity equalling powerlessness and self-loathing. What does this say, not just about our attitudes to food but to ourselves? Do we see ourselves as punished by food, enslaved?

The varieties of food available to us widens, bright, beautiful cookery programmes fill the TV channels and access to professionally produced food becomes easier and easier, but this ease, choice and colour was not reflected in the stories sent to us. Why were we sent so many of depressed middle-class women trapped in kitchens? So many abused women cramming their mouths with food, eating rather than fighting back? Women are clearly absorbing the concepts of 'good' and 'bad' food deep into their bones. The stories were soaked with guilt and shame. We wanted our collection to recognise this fact, but as a women's publisher, we made the difficult editorial decision that we would not publish a collection of 22 women victims.

Making the final selection, we chose stories that reflect these hostilities and fears, but balance them with confidence, humour and defiance. The title story, Gill Brightmore's 'The

Woman Who Loved Cucumbers', takes obsession to its outer limits. Jenny Sullivan's 'Cymer Tarts' questions the emotions that might drive over-eating. Sue Morgan's 'Anorexic Hamster' dramatises the awkward, apologetic way families struggle and fail with eating disorders. In Nia Williams' brutal 'The Fast' the refusal of food is a last, desperate rejection of life.

Many stories picked out the way food can be used for punishment or reward in families. In Janet Holcroft's 'The Sugar Pig', Gail Hughes's 'The Go-Go Man' and Melanie Newman's 'Pink Cake', 'treat' food is used to buy children's love, with varying degrees of success. In Penny Anne Windsor's 'Gaps', food is given and withheld as a form of sadistic control. In contrast, the narrator of Alexandra Ward's 'Retreat' is bullied by bad food and silence, but practised by strangers, this cruelty loses much of its power. Her story is comic and sharp – no victims there.

The daily task of feeding the family arouses a wide variety of emotions. Angela Rigby's hilarious 'Fred's Dinner' captures three different women's reaction to the job of 'getting dinner on the table', pinpointing the way women's feelings are changing. In Christine Hirst's 'The Cook', a woman uses food for revenge. Cooking for children, however, gives mothers a connection to their children, missed when it is gone, as in Lynne Rees's 'Home Cooking'. Liz Hinds' 'Laverbread' begins as a warm, affectionate portrait of the food of the narrator's youth, but grows darker, the move from sweet Welsh cakes to bitter laverbread mirroring the change from love to grief.

While many women felt trapped in the kitchen, men's cooking is a performance, a special occasion, as in Jo Hughes's 'Sunday Lunch with Oliver', or professional, like the chef in Julia Gregson's 'Ma Maison'. Many of our stories demonstrate to a degree the argument of Gregson's chef, that the preparation of food is too hard 'without love'.

Food connects us to those we have loved, to our pasts. The Sharon fruit in Chloe Heuch's 'Sharon' are a haunting silent memorial for a lost child. In Lindsey Ashford's 'Passion Fruit' two very different women share grief, remembered love and the bitter fruit.

Food is also seduction, escape, pleasure. In Christine Harrison's 'Coquette au Café' a woman reconnects with her ex-lover over cream cakes and plays with the idea of getting him back. One bite of the simple French pastry in Ann Morus's 'Mushrooms' reveals a whole new world for a young girl, changing her aspirations forever. In Imogen Herrad's 'Bronwerdd' the narrator is driven by magic and a lust for spinach. Our closing story, Siân James's 'Strawberry Cream', marks the moment where a girl leaves the bliss of chocolate for new adult pleasures.

It was noticeable that authors concentrated on domestic settings, with surprisingly few stories about eating out or the production of food. Several authors raised the issue of vegetarianism, represented here with Sarah A. Todd's deft fantasy 'Last Night's Dinner'. 'Bronwerdd' also reflects on the way life feeds off life. Both authors use fantasy, where, perhaps, a more realistic approach to the theme could get weighed down in self-righteousness.

The aim of all Honno's publishing is to give a home to women's writing in Wales, where writers and readers can find each other and feel part of a community. We are very pleased that this collection has been able to bring together the work of established, recognised writers, authors who are fast gaining a deserved reputation and some who are being published here for the first time. We are grateful to all the writers for their willingness to share their work with us, and to Gwenllïan Dafydd and Alyson Tyler at Honno for all their excellent editorial contributions and enthusiasm.

This anthology is dedicated to Gail Hughes, who sadly died of cancer in 2001.

Janet Thomas and Patricia Duncker

FRED'S DINNER

~

Angela Rigby

It started as the faint thundering of distant feet overhead. A door opened and crashed shut. It became a loud clatter of feet crossing a hard floor. Another door opened and crashed. Feet roared down the wooden staircase and were then muffled a little on the parquet hallway. The front door opened and crashed. Retreating feet died out on the concrete path.

Caroline and I looked at each other, suspending the unpacking of crockery.

'What was that?'

'Someone in a great hurry to leave the upstairs flat,' I suggested.

'Sounds odd,' said Caroline, 'I thought we had a quiet elderly couple overhead.'

'Perhaps it was an angry visitor leaving. Maybe it's the quiet couple's son and they've just had a row!'

'I think those were high-heeled shoes. Men's shoes don't clatter like that. And would a son be visiting in the middle of the day on a Monday?'

We continued unpacking. We had taken the week off in order to move into the downstairs section of the Victorian house as the 'professional young people' requested in the advertisement. It was perfect, including the shared use of the back garden with its neglected lawn, shrubs and clothesline.

At precisely the same time the following day the thundering began again.

'Quick,' cried Caroline, 'the front room!'

We shot into her bedroom and ran to the big bay window. The thunder developed as before and the front door crashed. An elderly woman exploded into view, her body inclined forwards as she ran, her hands clutching a double-decker arrangement of plates divided by one metal cover and topped by another. Travelling at speed, she continued down the path, turned right onto the pavement and was hidden from view by the variegated privet.

Caroline and I looked at each other.

After the same performance occurred on the Wednesday, Caroline, who has more cheek than I have, organised a plan of discovery. In the evening she went upstairs with a cup, planning to ask for some sugar. The door was opened by a man, small and dark and mean-looking, who fetched our racing neighbour. The sugar was provided and Caroline invited her to have a cup of tea with us the next day. To my surprise the invitation was accepted; the arrangement being for two o'clock.

'There's obviously cooking going on in the morning,' Caroline explained, 'so I knew coffee was out. It has to be after lunch.'

Mrs Fay Willis, as she introduced herself, arrived at two o'clock. She was in her late fifties or early sixties with hair that was already quite grey and slightly tinted with blue. Her face was creased into fine wrinkles and was a mask of white; although this seemed to be the effect of face powder. Her eyes were pale blue, as was her suit and matching shoes. There was a white blouse and large pearl stud earrings. It was as if she was fading into a mist.

I poured the tea and we started with the weather and basic facts about ourselves, while Mrs Willis looked slowly and intently around the room, and then at us. I felt the criticism of my rough jeans and sweater, and of Caroline's full length flowered skirt and long untidy hair.

'We heard you come down the stairs yesterday,' said Caroline suddenly and brightly, 'and saw you running down the path. You must have been in a tremendous hurry!'

I curled up inside at the direct approach, but Mrs Willis replied without any evident reaction.

'I was taking Fred his dinner. He's my husband and he manages the ironmonger's on the parade. I take him a hot dinner every day.'

I calculated that the ironmonger's was a hundred yards along the road and visualised her sprinting past traffic and pedestrians.

'That's nice,' said Caroline in a tone that indicated she was at a loss for a suitable response. There was a moment's silence.

'Couldn't he take sandwiches?' I suggested, also not knowing quite what to say.

Mrs Willis gazed at us.

'He needs a HOT dinner!'

'Couldn't he come home?' Caroline asked.

I realised that this was not a diplomatic subject to continue discussing, but my feminist friend was not going to let go.

Mrs Willis's gaze became stronger.

'He prefers to stay in the shop for the customers.'

'It must be exhausting running like that!' mused Caroline, despite my discreet attempt at signals to stop.

'He is my husband,' stated Mrs Willis, 'I have to take him his dinner.'

The gaze, which had already reduced us and our house-keeping to disorder, was becoming intense.

'Why?' said Caroline.

'HE IS THE MAN!' said Mrs Willis.

There are statements, which require the sound of trumpets and gongs, of organ blasts and altar boys furiously ringing bells. There are times when the call for prayer goes out from mosques and rings over the streets while worshippers go down with foreheads to the floor. This was one of those statements and one of those times.

'So?' said Caroline, 'What's that got to do with it?'

I was shrinking into my armchair, hoping that I was getting smaller.

'HE IS THE BREADWINNER!' proclaimed Mrs Willis. The trumpets blew fanfares and gongs boinged. The organ shook the foundations of the church and bells screamed. The cry from the mosque brought whole cities to their knees. Mrs Willis's eyes shone.

'I do like your suit,' I said quickly, 'It's a lovely colour!'

She diverted her attention and her expression switched off.

'Do you, dear? I do like a suit. I always tell my daughter-in-law she should wear a suit. But she doesn't listen. Young people should listen to older people.'

'Why should they?' said Caroline.

'Because,' said Mrs Willis. 'They know more. They always know more!'

'You have a son then?' I said.

'A son and a daughter. My son works for an insurance company in London and my daughter emigrated to Australia.'

After the door closed behind her and we heard the court shoes ascending, Caroline turned to me.

'Wow! She must have had sex with that skinny little man!'

'Don't!' I said. 'Don't think about it!'

In the weeks that followed I gathered that while Caroline was not popular with our neighbour I was okay or, at least, I was receptive to advice. During brief meetings in the hall, in the garden or on some odd excuse that brought her to the door I learnt a range of facts. I heard that she always told her daughter-in-law that the son's shirts must be white and freshly ironed for the office every day, and that his suits must be regularly cleaned and brushed. I also discovered that visits from the daughter-in-law were rare. One Sunday afternoon when I joined her at the washing line I noted, with surprise, that she was hanging up the cloths with which we had just spied Fred cleaning his car. She assured me that she also ironed them. Comments on our clothes were frequent. I really ought to wear a suit, or at least a nice skirt. A white belt would be better and why didn't I wear any jewellery? She could never go out without her pearl ear studs; she would feel undressed.

'I don't believe it,' said Caroline, coming in from the clothesline one evening. 'I said something about the baby clothes on the line next door and she told me that when her babies were born she got up every morning at six o'clock to do the washing so that she could cook Fred's breakfast before he went to work. I asked why he couldn't make his own breakfast, and you know what she said . . .' She dropped the washing basket, and conducted three beats in the air. 'One, two three . . .'

"HE IS THE MAN!' we chanted together.

'She'll hear us!' I said, killing myself laughing.

'Wouldn't you think he could at least have cooked his own breakfast when she'd just had a baby!'

'I don't think she could have coped. What would she have done if she had actually seen a man cooking breakfast?'

We thought for a moment. 'She would have died,' I said.

'It would have been like one of those computers in science fiction which self-destruct when they can't cope with an illogical statement.'

'Where does she come from? Where on earth does she come from?'

'From suburbia,' I said, 'probably circa nineteen fifties. Or her mother did, and the data was fed in. Then the system was protected against interference, the password lost or destroyed. Now press any key to continue!'

After a while the subject lost its interest. Our teaching jobs absorbed our attention and we began to have a social life at weekends, Caroline with the art teacher and me with various men. This development interested Mrs Willis who could be observed looking out of a front window as we walked home or got out of cars. When we met her in the hall or garden she would give us a coy smile, and we got the message that she felt we were getting somewhere.

It was a Saturday in June when Caroline and I were both at home. I was cooking lunch and she correcting homework on the table. There was the faint thundering of distant feet. A door opened and crashed shut. There was a loud clatter of feet crossing the hard floor. Another door opened and crashed. Feet began to roar on the staircase. Neither of us moved or even took any particular notice. The roar altered to a crash followed by two more crashes and a scream.

We rushed out of the flat. She was lying on the hall floor, making deep guttural breathing sounds.

'Phone for an ambulance,' I shouted to Caroline, 'run, quick!'

Caroline took one frightened look and then she was gone. I knelt on the floor beside Mrs Willis and listened as the breathing sounds died out. There were broken plates, meat, potatoes, two vegetables, a slice of sponge pudding and custard spread around her. The gravy of Fred's dinner seeped into the blouse and pale suit. It was what she had become.

CYMER TARTS

~

Jenny Sullivan

Blue Hawaii was on the other night. Every time I see Elvis on telly, it puts me in mind of Cindy – used to work next to me down Cymer Cakes. I used to squirt on the icing and splosh it about, Cindy put the cherry on, and Dilys next to her stuck 'em in boxes. Pretty, Cindy was: black hair, big brown eyes, fab'lous little figure, looked after herself, dressed nice, you know, but there was no side to her, neither, she was lovely. The maintenance blokes used to call her the Cherry Queen.

God, Cymer Tarts! When I started down the bakery, I could eat half a dozen of the bloody things, no problem, but after I'd been there about a week I couldn't look at 'em! We used to call ourselves that when we was on a girlie night out: The Cymer Tarts. Cindy never come with us, mind – no, I tell a lie. She come once, but only the once. She was all right early on, but once we'd got a couple of drinks down our necks, her nose went up a bit. By the end of the night, when we was all walking – well, staggering – home, clutching each other and screaming with laughter, like you do, you know, she just sort of disappeared. Scared someone would see her and tell her old man, I 'spect. Old Norman. She never said nothing, and she was still OK in work, but she never come out again.

He was old, her Norman. He must have been forty, forty-five, if he was a day, and Cindy was only our age, twenty-eight-ish. God knows why she married him. Pernickety old bastard if you ask me. Give up work because he had a heart attack. I thought that was why Cindy was working shifts down Cymer Cakes, till I found out different. Prob'ly because she didn't want to be stuck at home all day with him, partly to bring in a bit of extra cash to top up his Sickness Benefit, p'raps, that's what I thought.

We was icing and cherrying one day, me and Cindy (her real name was Cynthia, but everyone called her Cindy except Slimy Sid the foreman, who called her Sin) and we got talking about our blokes. Mine's no Sean Connery, don't get me wrong, but Cindy's old man was going bald and he bought her a Hoover for Christmas one year, which just about sums him up.

Anyway, when you're working, you can't look at people, too scared you might miss a tart with your icing squirter or lob a cherry on the floor, and so you sort of say stuff you wouldn't normally. Dilys next but one didn't, but Dil was definitely a couple of jam butties short of a picnic, if you get my drift, and she used to stand there humming to herself and sniffing. Which was another reason I didn't eat Cymer Tarts no more.

After a bit, I said to Cindy, 'How come you married old Norm then?' I could have said, 'How come you married that miserable old git,' but I didn't. I thought it, mind. Out the corner of my eye I saw her shrug.

'Dunno. He was there, I suppose. My Mam liked him, and she wanted me settled. And he went and asked her first, before he asked me, and by that time my Mam had already said I would.' She shrugged again. 'Seemed like a good idea at the time, and it got me away from Mam.'

Didn't sound much of a reason for getting hitched to an old bugger like that. I mean, my Derek's no Love God, like, but at least he's my age and we got stuff in common. And he never forgets to bring me a quarter of jelly babies on a Friday. And he certainly wouldn't never buy me a bloody Hoover for Christmas, I can tell you. Get it shoved where the sun don't shine if he did, and he knows it.

I decided to push. 'You happy, Cind?'

The cherry-popping figure next to me froze, thinking, and missed a tart.

'S'pose. Could be worse. He don't bother me much, you know, like that. He don't knock me about, so yeah, I suppose he's all right.'

I thought a bit about that. Then I said, 'If you could 'ave anybody, Cind, anybody in the hool world, who'd you pick? Me, I'd have Sean Connery.' There wasn't any hesitation at all. She come back with an answer fast as lightnin'.

'Elvis.'

'Elvis?' I stared at her. I thought she might have gone for Peter O'Toole, Richard Burton, even, someone a bit posh, like that.

'Elvis.' She let four Cymer Tarts slide past with no cherries. That would give Dilys a turn. I glanced up the line. She was wiping her nose on her sleeve, so she hadn't noticed.

We got talking, then, and it turned out that Elvis was her main thing. Honest, it was like throwing a switch! Once I got her started on Elvis I couldn't shut her up. She explained how she'd come to forgive him for marrying Priscilla, because she'd give him his daughter Lisa-Marie what was the apple of his eye, and anyway they was divorced now. She thought he looked better when he come out of the army, though he'd put on a bit of weight recently and all. She knew his favourite food was banana and bacon sandwiches fried in butter, which sounds disgustin' if you ask me, but. And then she got to the Dream. All Cind wanted out of life was to see Elvis Live at Las Vegas, since it didn't look like he'd be coming to Cymer any time soon. Turned out Elvis was the only reason she was working. She was saving to get to Las Vegas to see the King! Nothing to do with topping up ole Norm's sick pay. All she wanted was to see Elvis.

'That's why I don't come out no more,' she explained. 'Every penny I get I stick in my Elvis account down the Post Office. I gotta see him before I die, I *got to*. I hate these bloody cherries like poison, honest, but every cherry I put on gets me closer to the King. It's my dream.'

I squirted a blob of icing and shooshed it round with the nozzle. 'What does Norm think about it?' I asked.

'Norm? Who bloody cares?' she said, deftly dotting on a cherry. 'He don't know and I'm not telling him. I'm just gonna take my money, buy my ticket and go. He'll find out soon enough when his dinner's not put in front of him at five o'clock. Soon as I got enough for the plane ticket and the hotel, I'm off.'

I stared at her. She was gazing dreamily into space, Cymer Tarts gliding past in a steady, un-cherried stream.

'I bought this gorgeous silver dress, special,' she went on, 'down Cardiff. When I tried it on it sort of shined like fish scales, and it fit me like it'd been made for me. I got it all folded up in tissue paper in a box hidden down the back of my wardrobe. I'm gonna get to Caesar's Palace in Las Vegas, and I'm gonna have a bubble bath and put it on, then I'm gonna sit down at one of them little tables in that big room in the hotel right by people like Sammy Davis and Frank Sinatra and Peter Lawford, right down the front, and when Elvis comes on stage he'll see me in my shiny dress and then I'm gonna look mysterious at him.'

I turned to stare at her and missed another tart. She was miles off, dreaming, honest.

'An' if Elvis just looks at me, I'll die a happy woman,' she said. 'An' if I could just touch his hand, I'd prob'ly die right there, straight off.' She looked at me, seriously. 'He does, you know. He touches people, sometimes.'

Well, he was all right, Elvis, but he was better when he just started, when he was a young kid with sideburns. He'd got a bit on the fat side by then, to be honest with you, and tarted up in them shiny all-in-ones he looked like a lurex liver-sausage, right? Still, a girl's gotta have her dreams. We used to wind her up a bit after that, but somehow, once we knew she had this dream, we liked her more for it. Made her a bit more special, like?

Then, of course, the bastard went and died. No, not Norman the Hoover-giver, Him. Elvis. Keeled over while he was sitting on the bog and died. Fell off onto his knees with his nose on the carpet, and his girlfriend found him.

Slimy Sid found out lunch-time, the day it happened. He was prob'ly having it off in his car as per usual with Charmaine the Bakery Bicycle, and he must have had the radio on, and heard the news-flash. Anyway, he come back and told me.

And I had to go and tell Cindy, didn't I? She was my mate, and I tried to do it gentle-like – after all, it was her dream, all gone, wasn't it? – but gentle didn't make no difference. She sort of sagged into a heap. Couldn't stop her crying. Went hysterical she did, laughing and screaming. I know I should of slapped her face, stop her like, calm her down, but I couldn't bring myself to do it. Anyway, she was chucking herself about, and waving her arms, and there was Cymer Tarts flying in all directions, and icing squirting out of the hose because I hadn't thought to turn it off, and glassy cherries all over the floor, and Silly Dilys squawking like a headless chicken to add to the noise.

We got Cindy calmed down in the end, but it took ages,

and they had to shut down the line and we got all behind on the tarts and I had to stay behind and ice and cherry, both, until we'd caught up, while Sid took Cindy home.

Remember I said how pretty she was, Cindy? Lovely little figure and all? Well, that changed. Her dream was gone, see. It was like it wiped her out. She didn't have nothing left to live for. Now, not everybody agrees with me, but I think she done it deliberate. Killed herself, like. Oh, she din't take poison or hang herself or jump under a number forty-seven bus, nothing like that, but all the same, she done it.

D'you know, it gives me a weird feeling just thinking about it. She took all that money she'd got saved to go to Vegas to see Elvis – and she ate it. She used to bring in these huge packed lunches full of chocolate and cream cakes and bacon butties, stuff like that, and then she'd go down the canteen and have sausage, egg and chips as well. She started to put on weight, and still she ate and ate and ate. She got fatter and fatter until the legs on her were like upside-down milk bottles, quart ones, and she had to walk spraddle-legged, she was so huge. She used to nick tarts off the line and eat them when she thought nobody was looking. She got bigger and bigger, and still she ate. Her big brown eyes went piggy into her great moony face, and she had more chins than a Chinese phone book. She used to get fish and chips on the way home, I know because I seen her do it, and eat them out of the paper, and then she'd go and eat gravy dinner with her old man. I read something the other day in *Woman's Own*. Comfort Eating, they calls it. Honest, she was the size of a house, and that's what I reckon she was doing. Comfort Eating.

And it turned out so weird, in the end. Norman had to go into hospital, and the milkman went there one morning and saw there was already four pints of sour on the doorstep and put two and two together, like, if a bit belated.

When they broke down the door, guess where she was? She was on her knees and face on the bathroom floor. Well, in the lav, actually. Dead. Just like Elvis. Only where he'd been knee deep in pill bottles and syringes and drugs and stuff, she had boxes and boxes and boxes of Cymer Tarts, everywhere. All empty.

I bumped into her old man a week or so after the funeral. It was horrible, the funeral. The coffin was so bloody huge every time I looked at it I had to bite the inside of my cheek, not to let out a snigger. I couldn't seem to help it.

Anyway, Norm was looking old enough to be her grandad, and I wasn't going to speak, I was a bit embarrassed like. But he spotted me, and he give this watery little smile. We had a bit of a chat and I said how sorry I was, the way you do, you know, and next thing I know he's knocking on my front door that night with a parcel in his hand.

'She'd of wanted you to have this, Cynthia would,' he said, shoving it into my hands, and then he turned round and walked away, quick.

I looked at the parcel in my hand, couldn't work out what it could be. So I opened it, didn't I. Wished I hadn't, after. It upset me good and proper, and I never put it near me. It's down the back of my wardrobe.

All wrapped up in tissue paper, it was. A tiny, shimmery, silvery, expensive dress, that gleamed like a mackerel fresh out of the sea. Cindy's dream dress.

A dress fit to capture a King's attention.

GAPS

~

Penny Anne Windsor

'Come and join us.' His eyes are bright with hate.

The child is already eating a large slice of tortilla. Stuffing it in her mouth.

Ella imagines the taste, the smooth texture of the eggs, the heat of the potatoes. Imagines swallowing it.

The cicadas mount a chorus. An angry sun skids into the horizon. The heat encompasses the village like an armpit.

*   *   *

'I'm just phoning to tell you she's unstable again. Ranting, I'd call it. I don't know what possesses her. She obviously needs help. And it's harming Josie. She's only three but she understands what's going on.'

There is a pause. Ella presses her ear to the door.

'Well, thanks. I know that's an option but I'll try to cope for a bit longer.'

Jason makes several such calls every day. Every time Ella speaks, which isn't often, or moves to another part of the house. Which isn't often either. Less and less.

Not since the business of the notes.

Ella watches the rain sweep down from the mountains to the sea. A neighbour hurries along the pavement immediately outside the house, a cardigan pulled over her hair.

LOOK AT YOURSELF
BEAUTIFUL BUT FLAWED

UNFIT TO BE A MOTHER
THERE ARE PLACES FOR WOMEN LIKE YOU
POPULAR? – ATTENTION SEEKING
I WILL NEVER GO AWAY

On the doors, the windows, on books and saucepans, even on the toilet seat.

Ella goes to the bookshelf. She removes a hardback copy of *Jane Eyre* and a file she uses for newspaper articles which catch her attention—

The rebels fighting in the mountains.

A debate on the future of modern art.

The Other Andalucia.

Behind is a packet of brown ryvita, a small bottle of marmite, a tub of natural yoghurt, a carton of fruit juice, a mug, a knife and a spoon.

*   *   *

Ella watches them eat in hot air, thick as soup.

The sun has stolen my child, she thinks. The moon has stolen my child. The father has stolen my child.

Huyes, sol, sol, sol.

Huyes, luna, luna, luna.

Huyes padre, padre, padre.

You run away with my child.

mi niña, mi niña, mi niña.

He has taken her into the shifting shadows where the light plays tricks. He has taken her to a land of stories where all the women are black witches and all the mothers are mad.

There is one lemon hanging over the river path and, farther down, where the river splashes over the waterfall, some soft warm figs.

That's all. The village is poor. There is no plenty. No surplus.

'Josie must eat properly. She must come first,' Jason says.

Ella looks at the cows with their ribs bursting through their skin, climbing like goats in the hope of high mountain grass.

'Of course, Josie's our first priority.'

*   *   *

Prioritise.

Put it on the back boiler.

Meetings, agendas, visits, contacts, influence, persuasion.

Ella remembered those jobs well.

Decaffeinated coffee. Salad rolls.

Selling charm. Chairing. Charming.

A Pound of Flesh. A Pound of Charm.

*   *   *

'All right, since we're stuck here, every fortnight for four days, we won't eat – anything.' Ella feels wine-confident.

'We'll smoke, have the marijuana tea?' Jason sits with his face turned away from the fire.

'And the bottle of montilla, ' he adds.

'I suppose so.'

Later, in the hot tent, she turns, too restless to sleep.

He whispers in her ear. 'When, then, when do the four days start?'

Dreams lick her eyes.

'Tomorrow.'

*   *   *

Ella spreads the marmite carefully on the ryvita and wipes the knife with a tissue. She presents the plate to herself. She fills the mug with orange juice.

Jason picks up the phone.
Ella's throat curdles.

*   *   *

When she drinks the montilla and does not eat, she feels dizzy. When she floats in the river, the montilla, like a surfacing fish, appears in her throat.

'Do you feel OK?' she says to him on the third day.

'Fine.'

No affect.

Jason shuts his eyes.

Ella does not want food. She wants sustenance.

Without a dictionary she doesn't know why the difference in the words matter.

She can smell montilla and smoke on his breath.

It's late evening.

'She's asleep.'

'Yes.'

'*Now.*'

She feels his penis jabbing into her back.

'I want to sleep.'

He pulls her over. Like tossing a pancake.

She's as dry as the land but he takes her anyway, pleasured by her resistance.

'Bitch,' he says, 'you can't take it, can you?'

Jason, poor boy from the Bristol overspill estates, proud of his survival, contented, falls asleep.

Ella, from a nice part of town, sits by the dying fire, wrapping her guilt around her, listening to his breathing.

*   *   *

Long ago, at least it seemed long ago, in that land when she thought they had made friendship into love, Ella remembers they talked.

She can't remember what was said.

Then she was pregnant.

And Josie was born.

And that was that.

It was not that he doted on the child in the usual sense. But she was out of his control. Not in his plans. Hadn't been meant to happen.

So he fretted about her input and output. Measuring.

'I saw you use that knife for the dog food.'

'It's clean.'

The knife clatters on the kitchen floor next to her face as she falls.

'You took her out without my permission.'

'You left her in her playpen.'

'You're not feeding her the right way.'

'She needs more milk. She's choking on your milk. She needs a bottle.'

She needs. He needs.

He needs to study for his degree. Which he does not want. In case he becomes middle class and cannot plead Poor Boy from the Wrong Side of Town. While longing, at the same time, for the Nice Part of Town.

He studies late into the night, making a meal, maybe at midnight. Not allowing her into the kitchen. The meal or nothing. Bleating that she wants to make him middle class. Bleating like baby Josie.

Ella feels her breasts spouting milk like a fountain. Josie chokes. Ella feels her breasts choke with untapped milk. Like tight peach skins. The milk curdles. Josie, now on a bottle, continues to choke.

Ella hides ryvita and marmite and yoghurt behind *Jane Eyre* and refuses the midnight meal. He props up the child in a high chair and says, 'Come on, little darling, one more spoonful. Daddy loves you.'

Josie's eyes widen and she swallows her fear.

Ella questions the 'love'. 'Friendship into love'.

A platitude.

She attacks the crispbread, not bothering with marmite, and lets the crumbs fall on the books.

Sustenance – nourishing quality

foster

cherish

Food – victuals, nourishments, provisions

be – for worms, dead

be – for fishes, drowned

Ella tries 'lust'.

Lust – animal desire

lascivious passion

Love – hold dear

Friend – one joined to another in intimacy and mutual benevolence. person who acts for one.

Obviously whatever it was, wasn't love. Isn't love. Food seems the nearest, with the gaps and the bits about death.

*   *   *

They call them 'free days'. One looks after Josie, the other does as they please. Or as much as one can do as one pleases with no money!

But Jason no longer takes free days. He has to stay close to Josie to protect her from Ella. Who cannot be trusted. He doesn't say so in those words. He says so in many other words.

'Mood swings.'

'Neurotic behaviour.'

'Selfish.'

'Irresponsible.'

'Furthering your career at the child's expense.'

What career?

She taught a bit here and there. Occasionally had an exhibition. Occasionally even sold a painting. But The Career – of the meetings, agendas, contacts and charm, the last post as Community Education Officer for the county, she had long ago given up.

For all the right reasons.

To think.

To paint.

To wander.

As a release from salad rolls! Oh the irony! Then she had longed to sit down to a leisurely meal.

Ella imagines a round table of polished oak, with candles, a freshly cut salad in olive oil, a dish heaped with lasagne, the cheese spilling over the edges, a glass of white wine.

The picture swims away in the heat, following the river upstream to the hottest place of all where it goes underground and the white rocks crawl with red spiders.

Ella has left the tent early that morning. Even then it is hot.

Jason snores. They have had another row. She knows that much, but punch drunk with rows, she cannot now tell one row from another. He, replete with anger, has of course, noted it all down.

When she finds the potatoes, she is jubilant. By the remains of a campfire, hanging on a carob tree. And a bottle labelled 'gin'.

She swills it round in her mouth and spits it into the river.

She remembers such a scene in a book. Don Quixote, she thinks. It *is* gin.

Ella dances as the heat roars.

She must take the offerings back. If there are rows and she cannot remember the cause, she is guilty. She must bring presents.

'There's no smoke without fire.'

'It takes two to tango.'

'You've made your bed, now lie in it.'

'*La vida no esta una cama de rosas.*'

She drinks some gin and watches a bright blue flower bloom in a crevice on the opposite rock. It teeters in the heat. In the haze of the gin.

In the village her husband and child are already halfway through their tortilla.

Ella imagines the taste, the smooth texture of the eggs, the heat of the potatoes.

At home the carton of yoghurt, which she has forgotten either to eat or to throw away, shrinks under a blanket of mould.

She calls Josie's name and the name echoes in the gorge and comes back to her.

Well-fed, Jason and Josie return to the tent. Jason sprawls towards the child.

There really is no gap at all.

LAST NIGHT'S DINNER

~

Sarah A. Todd

Six months ago I came home from work and found a cow in my wardrobe. It's not as if it was trying on my Gucci hotpants or anything, but it was a shock all the same. I mean, don't get me wrong, I'm all for an element of hide in the modern girl's working wardrobe, but I prefer it not to be inhabited by the rest of the cow.

Still, there it was. Large as life, chewing placidly on the remains of a particularly nice silk scarf Auntie J. had brought back from Italy for my last birthday. A cow.

Cosmopolitan prepares a girl for a great many things in life. What to do when there is a large farmyard animal in her closet is not one of them. I tried saying 'shoo' a few times but the animal just stared at me and sniffed my leather skirt accusingly. Later, I realised that telling it to shoo was a little pointless anyway. How far could it go? My flat's very small. It's also on the fourteenth floor. I have trouble getting *men* up here, how the hell had I managed an entire heifer?

I paced round the bedroom for a while trying to think straight. How had a cow got up the stairs into my flat and taken up residence between my shirts and thigh-high boots? Could it levitate? Did it know how to operate a lift? How did it pick the lock? Was I dealing with the tormented genius of a cow-Houdini?

I turned to look at the thing. It was a small, brown-and-white variety (forgive me if I'm not exactly *au fait* with cow breeds) and seemed quite young, but such details paled into

23

insignificance compared to the undeniably freaky fact that the cow was translucent. Peering at it, I realised I could see straight through it to the back of the wardrobe, where my favourite Galliano linen shirt was fighting for breath as the bovine intruder's buttocks squeezed it against the shelving unit. I don't know if you've ever come home from a busy day at the office to find an ethereal farm animal grazing among your clothes, but in spite of my natural faintheartedness, I felt it merited closer investigation. Edging forward, I closed my eyes, reached out a hand, and attempted to stroke the animal's nose. It was further away than I thought, and it wasn't until my hand made contact with my linen shirt that I opened my eyes, thinking that the cow had moved. Translucent wisps of brown and white hide surrounded me. I had stepped right into the middle of the animal. The cow was a ghost, and as my hands dropped to my sides they fell through its skin and hung limply inside what should have been its carcass.

The cow turned its head and mooed at me.

Don't quote me, but I'm pretty certain that this was the point at which I screamed.

The rest of the evening passed in a drunken haze. I'm the kind of girl who likes to take life with a pinch of salt, a slice of lemon, and a shot of tequila. Boy did I down a few that evening! I even watched a few installments of Jerry Springer, but since none of them tackled the harrowing topic: 'So, you've got a cow in your closet' not even Jerry was much solace. It was a tough decision, but I was going to have to do what I vowed I would never do again, no matter *what* situation I found myself in.

I phoned my mother.

'Mum, there's a cow in my wardrobe.'

Silence at the end of the phone, then, 'A what, dear?'

'A cow. You know, large animals, give out a lot of milk . . .
um . . . go moo?'

'In your wardrobe?'

'Yes, Mum.' Curiously enough, at this point the absurdity
of the situation finally hit home. Trying to convince someone
else of the cow's existence made me doubt it too. My phone
is cordless so I was able to walk into the bedroom and check
for myself. The animal was still there, nuzzling against the
shoe rack. I took a deep breath.

'Mum. There is most definitely a cow in my wardrobe. Yes,
Mum, I have been drinking. No, I've never hallucinated
about animals before. All my most regular fantasies are most
definitely non-bovine related!'

'What are you going to do about it, then?' my brother,
Andrew, asked a week later. Mother had not been a lot of use.
Neither had either of my sisters, Jenny my best friend, Auntie
Jemima, my cousin Pip, the milkman or various assorted nice
people on the end of the Samaritan's helpline (including the
one who very audibly muttered 'We've got a right one here').

'I have absolutely no idea,' I confessed. 'I suppose I could
always start some sort of afterlife petting zoo.' We were
sitting in my kitchen making BLT's for brunch, and Andrew
was being more than usually helpful. I still had absolutely no
idea why a cow should want to take up residence in my
closet, but the thing had refused to budge for eight days and
it didn't seem to be causing any bother. It had learned to
move if I wanted any of my clothes. On Wednesday it had
been joined by a couple of chickens, which made me feel a
bit guilty about having McNuggets for lunch.

'Pass the bacon over, fatty, I want another sandwich,'

Andrew ordered with his usual charm and wit. Resisting the urge to throw the bread knife at him I reached for the frying pan. Straddling the gas hobs, a round, pink pig was nosing the remaining rashers mournfully. I could tell that Andrew had seen it, too, as his jaw dropped a good six inches.

'Abby, this is ridiculous,' he blurted. 'At this rate you'll be able to open your own farm.'

I turned off the heat and left my half-eaten BLT on the plate so we could go into the sitting room and consider the situation. There was a cow in my closet, accompanied by two of its little chick friends, and now I had a pig in my kitchen. Andrew was peering though the door of the kitchen, his eyes flicking from the stove to the pig and back again.

'You know when this cow appeared,' he began, 'you can't remember what you'd had for lunch that day, can you?' I thought carefully and had to admit that although I'd meant to keep an eye on the calories to get back into my favourite slip dress for cousin Katie's wedding, I had succumbed to a burger on the way home.

'Oh, that means that I've done fast food twice in one week!' I gasped. 'I had McNuggets at lunchtime today as well.'

Andrew was beginning to piece something together. 'Sooo,' he mused, 'you have a burger and a cow appears in your wardrobe. You have Chicken McNuggets and all of a sudden the cow has some feathered friends to keep it company. And then, when we're in the middle of some very tasty BLTs . . .'

He didn't need to finish. 'Great,' I muttered, 'I'm being haunted by lunch!' I had visions of my little flat becoming increasingly cluttered by the ghosts of whatever I had snacked on that afternoon. Tuna fish swimming happily in my bath, chickens roosting on my bookshelves, maybe a few more cows to keep the one in the wardrobe company. There had to be a solution, and cleverclogs Andrew thought he had it.

'It's quite simple really, sis. You go veggie for a while, see if they go away.'

I couldn't believe he was suggesting this. I'm a girl who *loves* her meat, and when I say that, I mean *loves* it. Quarter pounders, raw steak, chicken sandwiches, even the occasional slice of veal (just don't tell the bunny-loving freak I share an office with). The thought of giving it all up, even to avoid becoming the proprietor of a graveyard menagerie was . . . well, it was too awful even to contemplate.

'Surely not *all* meat?' I pleaded. Andrew shrugged.

'It's either that, or play Dr. Doolittle to all the little animal ghoulies.'

I sighed heavily and resigned myself to a lifetime of lentils and tofu. I didn't even know what tofu *was*, but I sure as hell didn't want to develop a meaningful relationship with it. Andrew hauled himself out of the couch and made a move to get his coat. 'I'll leave it with you, Abs. Thanks for the BLTs, but I think they've disagreed with the kebab I had last night.'

'Kebab?' I asked, following him as far as the kitchen.

'Yup.' He grinned sheepishly before disappearing through the door. 'Night out with the lads, you know what they're like.'

I put down my coffee cup and wandered back into the sitting room. There was a ghostly cat sitting on my sofa.

Six months on, things aren't so bad. I sort of got used to sharing my flat with a few ghosts, though it makes it more difficult to bring men home. A few weeks back quite a promising prospect was scared off by the cow jutting its head out of the wardrobe at a very inopportune moment. The cat likes to scare my parents by jumping up onto their laps from underneath them, but the chickens were quite well behaved, till they disappeared that is. That's the funny thing, really. The longer I've gone veggie, the less real they've become. Even the cow is beginning to fade. In a few more weeks it'll be little more than a wispy outline. If it weren't for Andrew coming round every now and again, I would probably have lost the cat as well.

Only thing is, I've begun to spot carrot tops growing in my slippers, and I'm sure that last Tuesday I saw bulgar wheat sprouting on the bathroom mat . . .

ANOREXIC HAMSTER

~

Sue Morgan

Hello.

Yes, it's me.

No, what did you think?

Of course I'm on my own.

They went yesterday. He picked them up. He said if I wanted I was welcome to go over, you know, tea-time, for mince pies, cake, take them their presents.

No, I gave them yesterday. It was up to them if they opened them or not.

They didn't. Took them with them in a black bin bag to open this morning.

No, I'm OK.

It just feels very strange, you know, dislocating, like part of me is missing.

They were excited, keen to get there, for Christmas to begin.

You? Having fun?

No, I know, I don't mean fun, but the kids, are your kids having . . .?

It's always a let down, I remember that so well, don't you?

I know, it is harder for you, they're so far away, yes, you hardly see them, I know. I can imagine it. You must.

But nothing ever comes even half way to what can be imagined, does it? Like a longed for pleasure, or an imagined taste, a dreamed of happiness, nothing can come up to . . . that level of perfection.

I know. Doomed to disappoint.

A wobbly? Tantrum? Has she done that before?

Over-excited.

What? Rescue remedy?

Is your, is Karen into all that?

Perhaps it's a lesson for life, you know, not to expect too much.

No, I'm not depressed, do I sound depressed?

I'm not. Just thoughtful. House empty, time to think.

No, I don't feel sorry for myself. Lots of people are alone over Christmas, I know. I know.

Don't be stupid. What could I have done? Gate-crashed someone else?

No, I didn't cook.

I can't cook for one.

No, I saw Jane Clarke, you know, my kids went to her for piano lessons.

No, they just stopped, hated practising.

Not her, she's nice.

She's quite a lot older than me.

No, she's Jewish, no, they're grown up, in Israel or America. She was married. It's her married name.

I don't know. I never asked.

She was in the supermarket looking out of place, like me, with a tiny half-filled trolley next to all these juggernauts, all these families stockpiling for the four days, you know, like there's a war on. Packets, boxes, cartons, tubs, it turns my stomach.

I just think of the waste.

We went out.

Pizza.

Yes, they do open on Christmas Day.

Perhaps they're Muslim Italians.

Tomato and mozzarella, basil.

Garlic bread.

House red. Half bottle.

No, she wasn't, she's got cystitis, she had mineral water.

No, she is good company, don't be cruel, you don't even know her.

Don't be cruel.

No, I'm all right. A bit maudlin.

Missing the kids. Missing you.

What about you?

What, on your own? Didn't Ben want to go with you?

Oh, I see.

It snowed?

You didn't over do it?

I mean, you don't normally run that far.

No, it's probably because of the snow. It makes you feel good, doesn't it? Zippy. It's full of minerals and positive ions.

From my gardening books.

I love it!

Sorry darling, I forgot to say, no, I really love it.

No, I know, but I'd never buy it for myself, not hardback and it's just what I wanted.

I've just dipped, not properly.

Not yet. Later tonight, in bed.

You like it? Well, it was hardly a surprise. Thought it might make you laugh. I'm hopeless, keeping things a secret.

Yes, I will too. Of you.

Yes, I could, I could light a fire. Seems too much effort just for one.

I've got no energy.

Just drifting around, listening to the silence, waiting for you to call.

It gets dark so early.

I know, but it's only four days, you can't see a difference yet.

No, you're right, a fire. It's a good idea.

Why don't we do that next year, go away, a cottage with a log fire?

I don't care, somewhere remote, away from all this, all this noise and fuss, buying and cooking and eating.

Yes, I've heard of one, no electricity.

Gas lamps.

Mention it to Karen, give her advance warning.

Oh.

The kids.

No, I hadn't thought.

Well, a few days some other time perhaps.

They may not even let it in the middle of winter.

I'll try and find out. No, it's not big enough for all the kids, and if yours come what will mine feel?

I know.

I know, but they're not logical are they, for god's sake, they're only kids, you can't expect them to act like adults. Bloody hell.

I'm sorry.

I am too.

It's just sometimes I don't know what we're doing to them with all this, you know, long term.

Yes, I read it too, this month's theory.

Marginally, till I saw they were all so well off, I mean they weren't affected financially.

No, but it bloody well helps.

OK, I know.

You've got to go?

Oh.

No, I'm just frightened of losing your voice.

I feel like going to sleep and waking up when it's all over.

Imagine losing four days of your life.

No, I know.

So what are you going to do?

Well, if she wants you to watch the film with them, and you've agreed.

What's she doing?

Like old times, then, like happy families?

If you drink enough you'll fall into bed for old time's sake.

I'm sorry.

Now I'm being cruel.

Just don't tell me if you do. I don't want to know.

Of course I don't talk in opposites.

My god, if we start playing that game . . .

So what's the film?

Hang on, I want to guess. Not *Lassie*? She hates animals, your kids told me that.

No pets, they said. That's all.

No, he's OK, still alive.

I haven't let him out of the cage because I'm afraid of him going down that hole in the floorboards, you know, where the knot of wood fell through.

You don't think he could squeeze through?

I'm not so sure. I'd feel terrible.

No. I'll give him a piece of apple later.

I'm starving! I only realise when I relax. Now I'm talking to you. I've been so tense.

I'll go and raid the fridge. Home alone Mum.

First time at Christmas.

First time this long.

No, you were here, remember, you stayed?

Yes, yes. It was fun.

I hate that word.

Fun.

I keep thinking of them, sitting round at *her* house, eating together.

She's a good cook, everything has to be homemade, everything fresh.

I bet she was up at six getting the turkey in.

Home cooked Mama food. Nurture. She's into all that stuff. It makes me want to weep. Like I haven't been a good mother.

She thinks my kids are skinny.

No, I know, they're like me; they burn it off, nervous energy.

You should see hers: pudgy squashy arms, legs like tree trunks.

She'll be stuffing them now, making up for all the years I've starved them.

Like the witch in the gingerbread house.

She probably thinks I've got a problem.

You know, with food.

I mean, think of my hamster.

No, *my* hamster I had when I was a girl.

It died.

No, it was young; they live about three years, right? I only had it a year.

I had this thing it mustn't get fat.

My friend had one that could hardly move, I thought it was cruel, letting it get like that. She thought it was cute, called it Mr Tubby.

So I let mine out to run about, it was always getting lost. I didn't want to over-feed it.

Perhaps I starved it. I hate thinking about it, even now. Perhaps I killed it.

No, it was winter.

What? You mean hibernating?

My god, you don't think I buried it alive?

No, you can sense it, can't you, if they're dead, it was curled up tight like it was sleeping but it was cold, stiff, I jumped back with shock as soon as I touched it.

No, we were all into it. Dieting, counting calories. Exercising.

Healthy living? More like penance.

You think so?

Its heart?

I hate thinking about it.

Out of false kindness, yes.

Some kind of denial?

But at least I've told *you*. My dark secret.

Tell me what you're going to do.

Oh, yes, the film.

Well, it's not *Lassie*, is it? It'll be the *Railway Children*, I saw that was on.

I think of Karen being a bit like the older one, you know, Jenny Agutter. Beautiful but sensible. Posh English. What was her name? Roberta. I never knew anyone called Roberta, did you?

Like a Head girl.

Not so sensible? What do you mean?

I always think of her coping, in control.

I mean, she'd not end up like me, all the lights off, not cooking for herself, freezing to death.

Yesterday?

All the strain? What do you mean?

Yes, it is stressful being a single mum. But the kids are older now, can't they help?

She what?

Emma?

No.

If I'd known, I wouldn't have said . . .

Oh, god.

I see.

You found her?

What, her fingers down her throat?

No, I see.

She's so young. How long has it been going on?

Alone?

I mean, sometimes you hear of it, don't you, they do it with a friend, like a secret pact.

A form of dieting.

Refusal, yes.

So secretive.

No-one knew?

Karen must have noticed, I mean, something must have shown?

Awful, she must feel awful. You too.

So you didn't sit down to dinner, none of you?

She's down to what?

Why didn't you tell me?

I feel bad now, going on like I did. The things I've said!

It did?

Yes, it makes it precious. They're so precious. They're the important things, I know.

What a day. I've never known it feel so unlike Christmas.

You go. Watch the film. It might take her mind off things, make her feel a bit more secure.

Relaxed, then.

No wonder she was upset. You said she threw a wobbly.

She said that, did she?

No you're right, perhaps it would help.

Perhaps it's a cry for help.

What? Ask for a transfer? Move there? Too far from them, yes.

I can't say, love, I don't want to add any pressure.

It would seem selfish, self-centred. You know how I feel.

No. I'd probably do the same. You're desperate to try anything.

I think you're right. If she said that.

OK.

OK. It's just a shock, that's all.

Nothing like for you, I know, but I can still see her, last time she was here, remember, when we went to get the hamster? Still a little girl. She was in heaven, in that pet shop. I was like that. I loved the tubs of grain and the hay and straw, the feel of it all, the smell.

I will. I'll try.

I'll make something, I don't know, cheese on toast, salad.

Yes, there's a bottle.

You left one, remember? For your next visit. Rioja.

I'll open it.

It'll help me sleep.

OK, no, I know, you've got to.

I've kept you long enough.

No, I won't.

Of course not, have I ever?

I understand, love, no I do. I'd do the same. Try to repair, mend.

You put it down.

I need to hear the sound.

I always think of things I wish I'd said.

Love? Are you there? I just wanted to say sorry. I'm sorry. And I love you. Yes, OK.

Bye.

Bye.

THE FAST

~

Nia Williams

It lies on its back, scooped out, still alive, unfolding its livid map of organs on to the pavement. The limbs stretch out and pulse: the points of a bloated star. Conner stands over it, and his mind hovers between possible futures. His arms and legs shake, in mockery of the spectacle at his feet. A cold part of Conner's consciousness is calculating, weighing outcomes, offering him a choice.

Thin sounds of aftermath waver on the world's edges. Help, or at any rate attention, is approaching. So life can still regain its balance, then. Conner waits, and contemplates his options. One possibility is to make sense of what has happened. He is an intelligent man, sanity intact: it's not too late to translate this little scene into reality, cause and effect. He could rewind a few minutes, retrieve the person who was running, just now, a yard behind him, whose name he knew, only a split second ago. He could repair that second, and run through it again, run, without flinching, through its transformation – *her* transformation – from running woman, panting, blonde, irritating woman, throwing shrill questions at his back, into this mess. Conner knows what this would entail. His mind would not immediately mend that rift in time. It's not a matter of settling down to watch the action replay. It would take years. He would have to dedicate himself to long nights of searching, pushing his memory, his powers of invention, for he didn't, after all, see what happened with his own eyes. He would spend most of his life reassembling this moment of impact, fission, evacuation.

People are running towards him in a slower time. The jigsaw is coming together. If he doesn't decide soon, the picture will form of its own accord, leaving him with one missing piece and a lifetime's obsession. He's remembering. The rumble and sudden crash of engines above, the impossibly real, comically huge aeroplanes filling the end of the alley, rattling the café table. The exclamation, shocked and humorous, that wilted in his throat and the animal energy that hurled him, hurled his colleagues, boring Jack and the irritating woman – hurled them from the table, over smashed cups and chair legs, down the street, towards the market square, threw and dragged them and a hundred other workers and shoppers and tourists in an accelerating current of panic. Odd, he thinks, as the civilized wail of sirens mushrooms around him, odd that nobody ran in the opposite direction, away from it all. We all went with the planes, trying to catch them up.

The woman shrieking questions. A hoof in his back. Tarmac slamming him in the face. His memory snaps shut. He doesn't remember getting to his feet or his first sight of her – of it – on the ground beside him. He wonders whether he's injured. Somebody is grasping his shoulder, asking something. More questions.

Conner takes the other option. He nudges his mind and it tilts the other way. The narrative breaks; the connections fizzle apart, the creature in front of him, twitching its last, takes on its own surreal identity. It is a sculpture, a painting, an idea. He recalls the irritating woman's name. Hannah. Hannah Longbridge. God, that woman gets on his nerves, with her daft questions and hyaenic laugh. Hannah Longbridge, running a yard behind him, increases her speed, draws level, runs past him, past the shell of her own remains, across the square and into an unknown life.

Conner is on his knees, with a blanket round his shoulders. People are busy around him, efficient. He extends a useless hand. He thinks, 'It will be cleaned out, soon. It will be empty, scoured and dry. A parchment bowl. Retreating, in the dark, to calm bone.'

Conner survives for two days without food or rest. A faint headache signals his new detachment. He is maintaining control. He says little, answers no questions: he's guarding against a slip of thought or memory. He returns to his hotel and packs his bags. In other rooms, his colleagues are also packing up and getting out. They clench their teeth and hurry around, colliding in the corridors. They try not to bump into Conner. As he boards the plane home, it occurs to Conner that he hasn't seen boring Jack. He finds himself employing war-movie phrases. Maybe Jack copped it, he thinks. Bought it. Then he sings to himself, *Hit the road, Jack, and don't you come back no more, no more, no more*. He stops, feeling absurd.

On the plane, somebody offers him a mint, and he takes it. For a few seconds he enjoys the innocence of it, the sweetness, the banality of sucking a mint on a flight home. Then he's aware of its intrusion, its slither and slide in his cheeks, clattering against his teeth, rolling and glistening in the groove of his tongue. He spits it into his hand and it stays there, clinging to his palm, gathering in the flesh, while they fly over safer lands. There are journalists waiting at the airport, asking questions. He and his colleagues are hustled past, ushered into taxis. He settles into the back seat, watching pavements and walls ease away. As they merge with the city traffic, he prises the mint out of his hand and flicks it out of the window.

Conner's wife flings the front door aside and clamps herself around him, reclaiming him from the outside world. She is hard-eyed, long-faced with worry. His daughter, Nadia, lurks in the shadow of the stairs, her face set with resentment. She resents his part in this incident, his name on the news. She resents his passivity, his frailty, his trivial bruises and scratches. Conner thinks: I couldn't even manage a glamorous death. And yet, when Nadia turns away to avoid the necessity of an embrace, Conner feels the tug of pain between them, the yanking of an invisible cord.

'You should go to bed,' says Conner's wife. It's a rebuke. Her voice scrapes angrily. And suddenly Conner remembers tiredness, as a ghost pressing on his shoulders, and he agrees to try and get some rest.

Lying on his bed, blank as the curtained daylight, Conner detects a waft of – what? A familiar, repulsive smell that begins to draw the saliva back into his mouth and stir his stomach. His wife is cooking meat.

'Sheryl,' he calls to the ceiling, 'Sheryl!'

And he turns onto his side and roars through the closed door and down the stairs, 'Sheryl! NO FOOD!'

She stumbles up the stairs, carrying the stench of grease and scorched flesh on her clothes and hands.

'Don't make me any food,' says Conner, as she pounces into the room. 'Please.'

He turns onto his back again.

Sheryl stands by the bed in her apron, holding a spatula. She stares at her husband lying, straight as a board, on their bed. She looks bereft.

'I thought you'd need something, ' she says.

'No. No food. Not yet.'

After a while Sheryl dredges up a phrase from her emergency store of TV dialogue: 'Shall I fetch the doctor? Maybe she could give you something to help you sleep.'

Sheryl doesn't attach any meaning to the phrase, or to the 'something' that will help. But Conner considers the suggestion with interest. He's never taken sleeping pills before, but he believes they bypass dreams, plunge straight through the senses and burrow into oblivion.

'Yes,' he says. Then, as an afterthought, 'Thank you.'

Conner knows his wife is fretting. He hears her talking in the kitchen; he recognizes the anxious creak in her voice and Nadia's exasperated, mumbled replies. He would like to set her mind at ease. He hasn't eaten properly for a week – just the occasional dry biscuit or cracker – but he feels better, and stronger, than he has for a long time. He's crisp and tough, like an old piece of wood. With satisfaction, he monitors the veins as they wither in his arms. He senses the shrivelling of viscera. Soon there'll be nothing inside him that moves of its own accord.

Nadia is a vegetarian, and Sheryl won't buy meat for herself alone. So at least Conner is spared that metallic stink and sizzle. But still he prefers not to stay with them at mealtimes. He doesn't like to see his daughter fill herself with all that green and yellow liqueous stuff, all the sauces and the soups that continue their long progress within her, through the tangle of her, pumped and swilled and sprayed and slopped, keeping her mechanics at work. He keeps away, and he knows that Nadia, at least, is grateful. She hardly looks at him nowadays. Her eyes pass across him, with low-lidded contempt. If she must address him, her words fall short of him, or stray past into the air. Conner doesn't mind. He approves of her steeliness, and would like to encourage it. He wants Nadia to grow solid and shatterproof. He wants a marble daughter. But he sees the spots break through her chin and forehead, he sees the raw skin under her bitten nails, and Conner leaves the room.

When Sheryl and Nadia eat, Conner hides in the spare room and keys in his reports. He's taken up the offer to work from home for a while. 'Compassionate leave' his manager called it, as if he were in the army. He doesn't feel that compassion is required, but he's glad to have this break from the office. He's in no hurry to return to his desk, to fend off the awkward goodwill of his colleagues, or to breathe in the fog of steak-and-kidney, liver-and-bacon, that billows up through the air-conditioning from the canteen, every morning from 10 o'clock onwards. Once upon a time, Conner relished the canteen ritual. He was always first in the queue, holding out his plate for assembly-line dollops of stewed mince and mash. He liked to parade his open-mindedness, singing the praises of mass-produced food, its coarse and comforting flavours, its bland but ample servings. He fancied himself as a student of plain fare, a democratic foodie, and on his jaunts abroad he insisted on dragging his companions off the beaten track to dingy eating houses full of sullen locals. He'd been planning one such outing at the café, just before the attack. He'd been wondering how to avoid inviting that bloody woman along.

All that has changed. Now, Conner is baffled by the whole notion of meals, and especially by canteen lunches. The table-loads of job titles and status-holders, salary bands and cuff-links and long-term strategies, all fuelling up just to propel themselves through another six hours of the day. Work, thinks Conner, as he starts up the computer. That's what really matters. Reports, data sheets, screen-savers, mouse-mats, staplers, clean-edged papers. In the midst of all that, eating is an irrelevance. Worse – it is an obscenity, like the hair that sprouts, the coagulating sweat and snot, encroaching, threatening to engulf order, at the first lapse of attention.

Conner can no more eat lunch in a canteen than he could go naked into his quarterly appraisal.

Sheryl and Nadia eat and clear away evidence of their meals behind closed doors. Conner works on the computer in the spare room. For a few days he allows the letters on the screen to carry him forward. He allows his wife to bring him strong, black tea; this, he assures himself, will skim off his innards like rain off a rock. Sheryl is unduly pleased, and tells Nadia that Dad is on the mend. Poor Sheryl. Conner probably still loves his wife, but he's now obliged to regard her as a well-meaning stranger. He sets up a camp bed in the spare room, the more easily to delete the familiarity of her lines and curves. He's broken off the old intimacies and in-jokes, the easy affection. It's a necessary part of the elimination of their earlier selves, of their first passion, when he had wanted to consume her, absorb her, wear her under his skin, take mouthfuls of her smile, her earlobes, the soft flesh of her thigh and underarm. He discards this, the consumption and possession, the savagery and tenderness; he bundles it up and throws it out.

Conner works. His methods change according to his need, but he works every day. He gives up on the computer when the letters pause in their inexorable march from left to right, and begin to ripple and heave. Sentences take on characters of their own, the 'E's smile vindictively at him, and Conner sees shapes forming in the spaces between words. He tries pen and paper, but objects to the fluidity of ink. Eventually, he finds his solution in a raddled old pencil, its nib worn almost to the wood. He scratches the words, carves them on to the page. It doesn't look very professional, but they can deal with that in the office.

Sheryl wants Conner to seek help. He hasn't the energy to

explain that he's already helping himself and, for the sake of peace and quiet, he agrees to attend a self-help group. They meet in a school hall, eight of them, seated in a circle in the middle of a wide wooden floor that smells of feet. Conner sits tall and ridiculous among dead-eyed girls, some no older than 13 and vulnerable as glass. He listens to them hating themselves, wanting to take control of their lives, wanting to disappear. He feels sorry for them, wishes them well, but he doesn't understand them. Conner isn't weak; he's stronger than ever before. He has nothing in common with these children in pursuit of despair. He lets his mind wander, and pictures himself in a desert, baking into tiny, hard grains.

One day a letter arrives, forwarded from Conner's manager. The parents have written. Hannah Longbridge's mother and father. They've written to the company, not knowing how to contact Conner directly, to thank him for staying with it, with her, in those last few moments. They know it's a lot to ask, but they would dearly like to meet him, to talk to him, if he can bear it, about what happened that day. They need to know.

Conner goes to see them. As he drives there, he wonders mildly what lies to tell. He pulls in to their street and sees, watching at the gate, a tall woman with slightly protruding front teeth. He immediately recalls Hannah's inane laugh. Mrs Longbridge guides him into the house, clutching his hand, and Conner stiffens, fearing a show of emotion. The house is a small, 1970s box, designed with space in mind, but suffocated by pimply ornaments and billowing furniture. In the sitting room are Mr Longbridge and Caroline, Hannah's sister. Caroline springs to her feet with offers of refreshment, crab-hops into the kitchen and returns with heaped plates of sandwiches and chocolate biscuits. She arranges these on a low table. Mr Longbridge eyes her, weary in his armchair, resting his elbows on his knees.

They talk about Hannah and her job, how much she enjoyed working at the company, how she had looked forward to that first stint abroad, how well she was doing. They touch on details – Hannah dithering about how many sleeveless tops to pack, and whether shorts would be appropriate – but they quickly veer away, and move on to the incident itself. The killing is so much easier than the trivialities of the previous day.

Mrs Longbridge asks Conner to tell them everything he remembers.

'Every little thing,' she insists softly, 'even if you think you shouldn't.'

Caroline adds with haste, 'If it's not too hard for you,' placing a hand on her mother's arm, as a restraint or as appeasement.

The two women perch on the edge of the sofa, side by side, gazing at him as though they might catch a glimpse of their lost girl. Mr Longbridge lowers his head and blinks at his feet. Conner begins to recite his version of the day.

He takes them through the morning, step by step. Into the hotel breakfast room. Hannah ate a good breakfast, he remembers – cooked meat, salted fish, strong cheese, bread and jam, yogurt and honey.

'She always had a good appetite,' says Mrs Longbridge, pleased, 'when she was happy.'

Conner passes briefly over their morning meeting. Hannah's contribution, he lies, was particularly useful. Caroline nods. Conner takes them out of the hotel and leads them to the café in the alleyway off the market square. He sits them at the grubby table outside, and rehearses that day's order: herb tea for him and Hannah, American coffee for boring Jack. Then he pauses, clears his throat, prepares them.

'We heard the planes approaching. Didn't really know what they were. We saw other people heading for the square, and followed.'

It comes out like that, as neat stage directions, and he's almost finished.

'There was a flash. A noise. And it was all over.'

Conner screws up his eyes, pretending to scrutinize the scene for every last detail.

'One minute, Hannah was standing there, watching the crowd, the next, she was gone.'

The two women hold their breath, waiting. Conner turns his gaunt face towards them.

'She can't have felt a thing.'

His serenity convinces Mrs Longbridge and her surviving daughter. After a moment or two, Caroline begins to cry. Mechanically, her mother pats her back. Mr Longbridge reaches for a sandwich and munches it in rhythm with the pat, pat, pat of his wife's hand. Conner thinks of the stale bread in his mouth, the saliva, galvanized into action, soaking and softening, turning the food into itself. They sit, and Caroline weeps. Mr Longbridge takes another bite. Partially dissolved blobs of bread and ham are propelled without effort from his throat to his stomach. The glands set to work, retching gastric juices through the mucus, reducing the pulp into creamy fluid, funnelling viscous waves into the small intestine. He finishes the sandwich and licks his forefinger and thumb.

'Oh,' groans Caroline, 'Oh dear.'

And she wipes her nose with the back of her hand.

Conner clenches himself tight, against Mr Longbridge and his mastication, against Caroline and her leaking misery. He concentrates on the mother's stony grief.

'How was it?' asks Sheryl when he comes home. 'How were they? Was it awful?'

She's left a casual plate of crackers on the table, and doesn't mention it. Conner sees through the strategy but, in a sudden spasm of sympathy, he reaches for one of the crackers and dabs at it with his tongue. Sheryl takes care not to comment. Conner isn't himself. The Longbridge ordeal was more tiring than he realized. Before he can muster his defences, an image slips through. Nadia, as a baby, and Conner nuzzling her forehead, placing his lips against the cool wisps of hair, feeling the hot skull underneath. He used to play at nibbling her fat toes, nipping at them to make her laugh, pulling back from the brink. Sheryl monitors his progress with the cracker. She says,

'What were they like? The parents?'

Conner is distracted, and a thought catches him unawares. Mr Longbridge may have played similar games with his own baby girls.

Conner sighs, acknowledging defeat, knowing what will come. There will be experts to ease his body back into old habits. They will teach his heart and liver, his stomach and kidney to resume their labours. He will re-learn the endless sequence of fuel and waste, life and death. Soon, the first trickle of liquid compassion will moisten his pipes and fill out his crevices; and in its wake will come the memory of Hannah Longbridge, of her last running steps behind him, of her cracked body and urgent questions, settling into the dust.

THE SUGAR PIG

~

Janet Holcroft

There were two weeks to Christmas but the snow still hadn't come. Inside the branches of the tree she could see tiny, frosted cottages dangling on golden threads. There was the school house, a church and a windmill, each one twirling tantalisingly in a world into which she longed to climb. They were quite unlike the tin decorations on their tree at home. And shining under their filmy coats, the sugar mice and pigs, pink and white, were hanging just beyond her reach. She stretched out her finger and touched the angel hair, which stuck to her hand like cobwebs.

'You like my pigs this year, darling?' said Aunty Lenka at her shoulder. She felt her Aunt's hot, peppery breath on her face and the warmth of the large body that always smelt of perfume, unlike her mother, who only smelt of babies.

'I've never seen them before,' said Carrie. 'Where do they come from?'

'London, darling. Uncle and I go to see the lights. But I saved one for you, to take home,' and she slipped her hand under the tree into the drawer of her cabinet and pulled out a pig, fat and pink and shiny. Carrie held it.

'May I eat it now?'

'But vee have dinner soon, darling, ven uncle comes in.' She had never learned how to say some words properly. 'You mustn't spoil your appetite.'

'What is it this week?' She ran her small fingers over the pig's wrapping.

'Paprika pork and some of my special meringue for dessert. You like ice cream in it?'

'Yes! And the Bull's Blood too?'

'Yes, for Uncle Bill and me and a little taste for you, like ven I vas a little girl.'

Aunty Lenka was a Hungarian refugee. She met Uncle Bill during the war, in a London underground station. She had tripped and he had saved her. They had no children of their own, but they loved Carrie and one evening every week they played a kind of game where Carrie was theirs. Aunty Lenka collected her from school and took her home to watch the television. There was no television at home. Sometimes Carrie would make cakes or play in Aunty's little garden. Then, when it was dark, Aunty Lenka started to cook. Carrie tasted capsicums, garlic, spiced sausages, when all she got at home was stew and chops. And the puddings were fine! Uncle Bill would come home and get out his stamp collection. He had thousands of stamps with beautiful pictures on them and lots of Magyar ones. She liked the butterflies and wild flowers. Every week he gave her a tiny, shiny envelope full of stamps to take home to put in her own album. They bought her the album for her birthday.

They lived next door to her grandmother's house but last Christmas her grandmother had died and now the house stood dark and empty and Carrie never went inside. At Aunty Lenka's she felt close to all that was left of her grand-mother. If she peeped through the gap in the fence she could see into the kitchen. The old gas cooker was still standing in its corner and the same curtains hung at the window. There was the brush by the back door that she used to play with.

'Are you tired tonight, Carrie?' Aunty Lenka wasn't a real Aunt.

'I think so,' said Carrie as she gazed at the cellophane wrapper. 'Can I have just one taste?'

'Just vone then and then Aunty vill put it in the cupboard until Daddy comes.'

Carrie pulled back the cellophane wrapper and smoothed her finger over the sugary flesh. When she tried to bite it her teeth scratched on the gritty surface. She thought it would have been soft, like chocolate. She scraped some into her mouth where it softened and turned into syrup on her teeth. She knew her mother wouldn't like it.

'Now, Aunty put it away until later.' Lenka took the pig and put it in her apron pocket.

'Can I look at your shelves?' asked Carrie. Each week she longed to look at the wooden shelves in the recess by the fire that housed Lenka's treasures from home, all small items that she had managed to bring in her suitcase, from the special visits to see what remained of her family. There were only women left. The men had all died in the war. There were dolls, painted jugs, velvet slippers and decorated plates all standing on the blue and white cloth. Carrie loved them all.

'Some of those vill be for you, vone day,' said Lenka, although she had already bought Carrie clothes and dolls. 'And ven I take you home vith me there vill be lots more.'

The weekly dinner party, just the three of them, was the highlight of Lenka's life. Lenka loved to lay the table in the traditional way and use the Austrian napkins and the crystal. Bill loved Carrie too. He would never have his own child. When they took her to Hungary, they could pass her off as theirs for a whole fortnight. Lenka loved to cherish the child. Last birthday she had found the pretty white rabbit with a tiny bottle of scent between its paws. She wondered, at the time, whether the child's mother would disapprove. And then there had been the special cakes. She *had* to buy two – one a clown, the other a snowman.

'Is it time for *Take Your Pick* yet?' asked Carrie and Lenka smiled. She stroked the child's pretty hair.

'Nearly! Come and I'll put it on in Uncle Bill's room.'

Lenka bustled off down the narrow hallway to the extension, built next to the kitchen, which Uncle Bill liked to call his 'snug'. Furnished and finished in floral chintz, it had none of the Hungarian touches that coloured the rest of the house. Lenka was always too busy for television. The set stood in the corner by the gas fire in its mahogany case. Bill's large chair filled the other corner. Lenka plumped up the cushions in her husband's chair and switched on the set, which made a familiar humming noise as it warmed up. Carrie loved the television. Every week she observed the rituals. She climbed into the large chair by the light of the popping gas fire as Michael Miles counted pound notes and the gong donged.

Uncle Bill liked ladies. Carrie knew. They were everywhere: in magazines and on the walls of the snug. But the most interesting were pushed under the seat of the leather armchair. They were not ladies like her mother or Aunty Lenka. These were ladies who hardly wore clothes and leaned forwards with big red lips ready for kissing. She didn't like to look at the ones under the cushion for too long in case Aunty Lenka came in and found her. These ladies didn't even wear swimming costumes and sat with their legs up. Carrie had never seen people in real life doing things like that. It wasn't nice.

The adverts came on. This was the boring bit of the show. Carrie looked across to December's Lady on the wall beside the fire, all ready for Christmas in her red nightie that you could see through a bit. There was a white furry edge to the nightie and her big bosoms were pushing out at the top. Carrie knew Aunty Lenka hated them. Carrie leaned forwards and lifted the page to see what came underneath.

'Our little Carrie, here again,' whispered the voice from the doorway. Carrie leapt up in the chair, her stomach lurched and her heart beat faster. Light flooded in and Uncle Bill's large body seemed to fill the small room.

'Make room for one tired Uncle in that chair. I don't know, *Take Your Pick* time again. These weeks fly by.'

Carrie climbed onto the broad arm of the chair and the man's heavy body slipped underneath her. She noticed his red leather slippers that looked almost polished. Daddy never wore slippers. She knew that Aunty Lenka kept them ready on the fender in front of the fire so that they were warm for him to put his feet into. In his left hand he held a glass of deep golden liquid that smelt rich and mysterious. His right arm folded around her waist and pulled her closer to his fat stomach, held in by the lemon shirt. She could feel his heart beating. She liked to sit on Daddy's knee, which was big and boney, and she loved the smell of his pipe and the chalky classroom. It didn't seem right to sit on Uncle Bill like this and feel his gurgling, podgy stomach underneath her. But she couldn't say. She couldn't tell Aunty Lenka because she was so kind and, anyway, Carrie loved the dinners and being grown up. They never had Bull's Blood at home. Sometimes her eyes went dizzy, like when you twirled round too many times.

'Do you like my little ladies, Carrie? I saw you having a peep. They're only a bit of fun for a tired old uncle. Here, I'll show you a lovely black girl,' and he rested the glass on the left arm of the chair where it glinted in the gaslight. Uncle Bill leaned forwards to reach the calendar.

'July, she was, I think.' He took the calendar off the wall and turned back the pages. Carrie had slid sideways on his knee and his groping, fumbling hands wriggled around her bare thighs as he pulled her back on to his fleshy stomach.

Now his body felt far too hot and Carrie knew that this was all wrong and she didn't want to stay in his room any longer.

'No need to go yet, Carrie. Your programme's not finished. Let's see who gets the star prize.'

And she felt the hands grip more firmly around her legs.

The door opened. Aunty Lenka stood there in her apron, which was splashed with red juice, holding a tea towel. Carrie noticed her Aunt's face change and she bustled forwards and lifted her up into the air, putting her down well away from the large chair and the man who knocked the remains of his whisky onto the floor.

'Dinner's ready, my darling. Bill, turn that rubbish off and put the fire out.'

'Can't you be more careful, you stupid woman. Look what a mess you've made on the carpet.'

Carrie sat at the table and saw that Aunty Lenka wasn't smiling. They started with a yellow soup that didn't really have much taste. Carrie couldn't eat the bread roll. Then they had Paprika Pork, which was usually delicious, but this time it tasted too salty and Carrie had to leave most of it. The pudding resembled a white mountain, but Carrie just felt sick. She didn't have any Bull's Blood either. Aunty Lenka tried hard to make the evening special, but the magic did not work. Uncle Bill usually told her funny stories, but tonight he didn't look at her and drank more Bull's Blood than usual. They ate in silence. Carrie thought Aunty Lenka's eyes were wet when she carried in the pudding.

After dinner they sat by the fire and Uncle Bill produced the stamp album and the large envelopes, bursting with delicate colours. Some were rectangles, some were squares, some large, some small. Carrie usually liked to sort them out and place her favourites in long straight lines across the carpet. Tonight she just wanted to go home. She watched the large, dark clock with its golden fingers clicking slowly round to nine o'clock. There would be the knock at the door and she would leave.

Lenka carried the dirty plates and dishes to the kitchen.

She couldn't bear his hands upon her, scrabbling in the darkness, wanting satisfaction. But as a young woman she knew it was her duty and he had promised her a future. He had the money to pay for her return to Hungary, by special visa, every other year. The only pleasure in her narrow life was this child, like a gift. The child would never come again. She heard the knock at the front door and put on the usual convincing smile that took her through life, shielding her darkest secrets. God willing, the child wouldn't tell her mother and maybe she would forget and come again. Perhaps if she left things until after Christmas, buying a lovely little present of course. Carrie would forget.

George Morgan stood against the winter night, his black curls glistening with raindrops from the light of the house.

'Evening, Lenka. I'm not too late, am I? Only Gwen couldn't get the baby down tonight. I think he's got a touch of colic.'

'Not at all, George. Come on in. It's been a lovely evening. Bill is just showing Carrie the stamps.'

'He's ever so patient with her. She loves those stamps, I must say.'

And as they entered the warmth of the living room George Morgan was charmed at the sight of this middle-aged man giving so much time to his little girl. There was no grandfather now and Bill filled the spot. A perfect match. They were lucky and grateful.

Carrie jumped up from the carpet and wrapped her arms around her father's waist. She did not smile.

'Can we go home now?' she asked, looking up into his face.

'Yes, but not before you've said something to your Aunty Lenka and Uncle Bill.'

'Thank you.'

She didn't really want to say thank you.

'That is our pleasure, darling. Vee love having you. You must come again soon.' Lenka fumbled with Carrie's coat and hat, wrapping her up.

Just before Carrie left, Lenka remembered. 'Vait, my darling,' and she disappeared into the kitchen, returning with a small, brown paper bag. 'Your pig.'

'Thank you.'

Carrie held it tightly in her left hand. She didn't want to show it to her father. She didn't ever want to see the pig's pink body again.

They walked together in silence. Usually Carrie loved to stare up at the night sky while her father pointed out the constellations. Tonight she just wanted to get home, to return to the familiar things that were her real life, not the pretend life in Aunty Lenka's house. In her own house everyone could be trusted.

She knew what she had to do and it seemed, then, in the cold damp of that December night, the worst thing she would do in her whole life. As they rounded the bend by the sweet shop she knew that they would pass the bin. It stood against the lamppost on the corner, the light from above illuminating the brightly-coloured sweet wrappers that flapped in the night air. Her father was looking the other way. Without faltering in her step she raised her arm and dropped the brown paper bag into the bin. Her father didn't even hear the slight thud as it landed. There, she had done it. The pig was in the bin.

MUSHROOMS

~

Ann Morus

She was fifteen – out of Wales for the first time, on her own
for the first time, staying for three weeks with a family near
Poitiers on an exchange visit. Her mother had complained,
loudly, of the expense; her French teacher had said that three
weeks in France during the Easter holiday before O-levels
would give her a better chance of passing the exam, and her
mother had muttered sourly that if she'd been taught properly over the previous five years she'd have passed anyway.
Catherine could tell she would have to pay for this in every
future French lesson until the teacher found a new grievance.

Finally, after trains and a boat and more trains, she was
on another planet. The French family was polite but distant:
the parents' shoe shop had a cash-flow problem and their
daughter, expecting the English visitor to be tall, sporty and
full of jokes, lost interest when it became clear that Catherine
was none of these things, and not even English. Catherine
was on the whole relieved; she had enough to do in reacting
to her new surroundings (the people! the clothes! the shops!
the houses! the fountains! and above all, the food!). She sat
contentedly in corners or trailed behind them, feeling like a
poor relation but glad to have the opportunity to notice
without being noticed.

On the second Sunday the family went to a birthday party
for the father's cousin, in a village about thirty kilometres
away. There was a pretty garden, food in white serving-
dishes on a long table, wine chilled in what looked like a

water-butt, sunshine, brightness, warmth. After she had stood in line to give her polite congratulations, she moved from the terrace towards the long table; she looked at the chicken under mustard, the fish in aspic, the quiches, and planned to try all of them in turn. At home, her mother's idea of a good meal was to throw all the ingredients into a large saucepan, cover them with water, and stir vigorously at intervals for two hours; in France she had become aware of a new world of tastes. There was a tray of tartlets on the table near her, pale golden pastry enclosing mushrooms in a deep brown sauce – perhaps one of those before she let herself be drawn irresistibly to the chicken?

The mushrooms were rich and firm and plumply opulent; the sauce was creamy, smooth to the tongue and yet carrying a tang of something piquant beneath, distinctive yet impossible to identify. The pastry crumbled delicately on the tongue, nearly crisp and yet nearly moist, with a taste that was not quite sharp and not quite sweet. She had to have another, which was the same and yet in some indefinable way subtly different on her expectant and delighted tongue, and still with that tang under the creaminess that she could almost name, which meant she had to have another, and another. So it was possible, she thought, to be drunk on food when the pleasure was great enough. One more, just one more. And another. And another.

She read French (no other subject was ever likely) at the University of London. In the first year she lived in a hall of residence and visited her mother once a month; in her second year, she shared a flat with three other women students and visited her mother once each term. In her third year she lived in a flat in Tottenham with Derek, visiting her mother (who of course knew nothing of Derek's existence) only in the vacations, for a week at most; she was too far away from her younger life there to feel at home, and not far enough away to be merely a visitor. None of her friends, and certainly not Derek, was allowed to visit or phone her there. Her new, adult life was to be kept strictly on the English side of the *cordon sanitaire*.

On the last Sunday of the Easter vacation before Finals, Derek told her that she lacked commitment and had never been there for him, really, and left her for a trainee furrier from Godalming. When the exam results came out she was back in Wales with her mother: she got a II:i (noting with pleasure that Derek could only manage a II:ii). Hurt but free, she abandoned her plans (made with Derek, who was going to do the same course) of post-graduate training to teach French in Britain, and decided instead to teach English in France, a plan hampered by her total lack of any teaching qualifications and by the fact that all the promising jobs had been taken long before. Determined to do *something*, she took the only job she was offered, in Rabat.

Morocco affected her as France had on her first visit – she was constantly delighted by its difference from everything familiar to her – but her working life was less delightful. The hours were long, the work was difficult, and her low pay meant she lived in a small rundown house in one of the older quarters, but she was suddenly where she wanted to be. It was exotic, it was mysterious, it was *different*. It took her some time to realise that the difference she so much enjoyed was a wall of brass between her and the Moroccans she met through her work or in daily life: she was outside their language, their religion, their culture, their continent, and she felt she would never be able to reach them or truly to know them. Her colleagues, unfortunately, seemed all too easily knowable: too predictable, too boring, too (it was another

couple of months before she reached this conclusion) *English*.
She felt isolated, and not merely from friendship: an infu-
riating couplet kept running through her mind:

What men call gallantry, and gods adultery,

Is much more common where the climate's sultry.

Not here it isn't, George Gordon, she thought irritably as
she lay on her low flat bed.

In her second year in Rabat, two new teachers arrived
from Britain. Sandra had very blonde hair, very black eyebrows, came from Wolverhampton and clearly fancied Mark,
who was tall and thin with pale brown hair and came from
Wivelsfield in Sussex. ('Between Haywards Heath and
Hassocks' was always his answer when asked where
Wivelsfield was; it was never clear whether this was intended
to be a joke. His grin, however, was remarkably attractive.)
Rabat for two years was part of his career plan, so that he
could add Moroccan Arabic to the Egyptian Arabic his
degree had given him, and he would then return to Britain
to do a PhD on diglossia; Catherine admired this forward
planning while recognising herself to be incapable of it.
Recoiling from Sandra's eyebrows, he spent more and more
time with Catherine, who felt chosen and happy to be
chosen. His attention was flattering after a long time of
feeling seriously unflattered; it rapidly became clear that
she no longer needed to be alone on her low flat bed.

In the spring vacation they went to Marrakesh; they stood
with the crowd in Djmaa El Fna watching the snake-charmers
and Mark, looking straight ahead at the bored, sinuous snakes,
said that they could get married. And Catherine, thinking
of the alternative, said yes, they could. They married at the
end of that summer, in Haywards Heath Registry Office
(Catherine's mother was officially In Bad Health, and unable
to organise or even attend the ceremony). The week before

the wedding, which she spent with Mark and his parents, was deeply uncomfortable; not only were she and Mark not allowed to be alone together (still less to share a bedroom), but his parents, while behaving with impeccable surface courtesy, made it clear that she was a wily, near-foreign schemer who had lured their poor deluded boy into an early marriage and would thus wreck his brilliant career before it had even started. For a few days, her mother's attitude of open contempt for Registry Offices, weddings in general, and any man who wanted to marry *her* seemed preferable.

They returned to Rabat for the second year of Mark's career plan; Catherine felt that she was more strongly aware of being in her last year in Morocco than in the first year of her marriage. She realised that she loved the warmth and colour of the place, its sense of life, in spite of the flaws she saw in it; it had touched her and changed her, and she resented having to leave.

They moved to London. Mark began his PhD at the School of Oriental and African Studies, and Catherine got a job teaching English at a language school in Putney. Mark became absorbed in his work, only fully alive, it seemed, when discussing the precise dimensions of the knotty questions his research had arrived at. He began to bring home fellow research students – all of them English – for long discursive meals, and Catherine realised in humiliation that they preferred English nursery food (bangers and mash, liver and bacon hotpot, rice pudding, bright improbably-coloured jellies) to the French and Moroccan dishes she enjoyed cooking and eating (bstila, toujen, mhanncha, haloua rhifa – even to say their names brought pleasure). As time went on, her suspicion grew that Mark's tastes had changed; he had genuinely enjoyed Moroccan food in Morocco, but back in England he had now with a sigh of relief, reverted. She could see the food in her life stretching ahead of her, and she was bored.

Feeling more and more isolated she tried to contact friends from university days, but they all seemed to have moved or disappeared except Elizabeth, the flatmate she had liked least who never remembered when it was her turn to clean the bathroom. Elizabeth, it turned out, was married to an Italian banker twenty years her senior, and was living near Regents Park in such splendour that she would clearly never have to clean a bathroom again. Catherine enjoyed the friendliness of her welcome until she realised that Elizabeth was casually interested in the sort of life she herself had avoided; Catherine had been invited for purposes of self-congratulatory comparison. Her life seemed sadder and drabber than ever.

Increasingly she felt disconnected from everything around her; she began to think that teaching English as a foreign language was not necessarily what she wanted to do for the rest of her life, and that analysing imagery in French medieval poetry or exploring realism and romanticism in the nineteenth-century French novel would be far preferable. (She began also to wonder whether beneath the intellectual curiosity was the childish wail: if he can, why can't I?)

In bed one night she suddenly realised what Mark's love-making (and for him that was clearly what it was) reminded her of: it used the same techniques as her mother's cooking. Unfortunately this thought occurred to her during the process itself; she started to laugh uncontrollably and then seeing the concern on his face above her (as always), she managed to modulate the laughter into convincingly orgasmic cries. He seemed happy.

Afterwards, as they lay together looking at the ceiling, he explained in detail exactly which early twentieth-century texts created the problems which were delaying his research; Catherine felt a distant sympathy for him, as if a stranger had stopped her in the street and started to tell her his life-story. Mark pointed out that the extra time for his research would need more money to cover their fast-disappearing savings. Perhaps she could think about taking on some more teaching ? A few hours a week ?

Catherine turned on to her side away from him. Even disillusion wasn't what it used to be.

It was Massimo's birthday and Elizabeth had invited Mark and Catherine. Massimo's cousin Demetrio could tell Catherine about a few hours of English teaching soon to become available at one of the adult education centres where he taught Italian, and he might or might not be there. 'He can't help it,' said Massimo. 'He's half-Polish.' Elizabeth had lent Catherine a dress (one she herself, of course, would never wear again) a shimmering column of creamy grey that looked nothing on the hanger and everything on her body. Wearing it made Catherine feel not merely attractive but invulnerable. The chiffon was an armour.

She moved from one group to another, talking in English and French to interesting and interested strangers. After a couple of glasses of wine, her boring everyday self was left behind, and the irresistible wearer of the dress took over. She hoped that the unreliable Demetrio would not appear and compel her to talk about something as banal as a job; she so rarely had this sense of being at total ease with herself and her body. And then, at five minutes to midnight, there was a sudden commotion and raised voices in the hall, and a dark handsome man in black bounded into the room; an accompanying puff of smoke, she thought, and he'd have been the Demon King. Behind him was Elizabeth, looking irritated, and a delicate, heavily made-up blonde who seemed to wish she was somewhere else.

Elizabeth made for Catherine, the others following. 'Catherine,' said Elizabeth grimly, 'this is Demetrio. Demetrio, this is Catherine.'

Demetrio looked her up and down; the dress clearly made an impression.

'You wanted me to come,' he said to Elizabeth. It sounded like a challenge. 'I am late, but I am here. What is the problem?'

'Nothing,' said Elizabeth wearily. 'Tell her about the job.' She moved away, relieved.

Demetrio turned to Catherine. 'So, where have you taught English? How long? At what levels?'

She told him, curtly; he had broken her mood and she was irritated.

'That will be good enough, I think. Now, finish *that* –' he pointed to the drink she was holding – 'and we can talk about it.'

He put his hand under her elbow and guided her towards the hall; instead of going to one of the smaller rooms at the back of the house as she had expected, he opened the front door and guided her outside.

'Where are we going?'

'To talk about this job over a drink.'

'We can have a drink in *there*.' She waved towards the house where her clothes, her handbag and her husband were.

'But not talk so well.'

'The pubs are all closed.'

'But the clubs are not. Now –' he opened the door of a small black car – 'you like jazz, Latin, blues, what?'

She had no idea where the dark, smoky club was; the music was vaguely jazz, vaguely Latin. They sat at a corner table and drank vodka and he spent five minutes telling her about the job and the next two hours asking her about her life. She felt him concentrating on her with a single-minded energy and open purpose that was completely new to her. She discovered she liked it.

He drove her home through the empty streets. There was a light in the kitchen of their flat. Demetrio looked amused, said, 'Ah, your good husband,' and opened the car door for her. As she closed the front door behind her she heard his car drive away, and felt suddenly dull and flat and tired. Mark was asleep, head in hands, at the kitchen table. She wondered what had happened to the delicate, made-up woman.

In the following days Mark seemed to be waiting for her to talk to him about something – she had a sense of him ready to help and encourage her, to make everything easier, if she would only take the first step – but she had nothing to say. Gradually he stopped waiting, and his life less and less frequently intersected hers.

She got the job (Monday and Thursday evenings, seven o'clock till nine), but her attempts to settle into the new routine of her life were disrupted. Mondays were, thankfully, problem-free, but on Thursdays Demetrio also taught until nine, and he would sometimes wait for her and offer her a life home, which she at first refused until, feeling ridiculously prissy, she finally accepted. And after her dark imaginings, it was merely a lift home, of course, as instrumental as a taxi-ride – except that she knew it was not. And she wondered angrily what he was doing on the evenings he did not wait for her.

The pattern continued for the rest of the term. She started to hear something of his earlier life: the different homes and relations, the different countries, the different languages, the sense that all and none of them were his and that there was no one place where he belonged. She had never before met someone who perceived so clearly that wherever he was in the world, he would always be different from those around him, or who made the most of it so shamelessly, turning the fact that to someone like Mark he was a half-wop, half-polack, deadbeat teacher of badly-attended evening classes, into the quest of a Romantic wanderer, searching the world for the ultimate wonderful thing that would give ease to his restless spirit. He dramatised to an extreme degree her own feelings of not fitting in, and when she was with him she did not need to think about her own alienation from the life around her: he did it for her.

She knew that if she gave the slightest hint of a movement towards him she would be swept up and carried off, but she also realised that as time passed and the friendly distance she had established between them became more firmly entrenched, it became even more difficult for her to make a move. When she was with him, she felt the heavy pressure of his concentration on her like a weight holding her down; when she was not she felt able to breathe more freely, but also bereft and dull. I should have slept with him at the beginning, she thought; he'd have lost interest in me by now.

Mark was happy; his research was going well and he was glad she was making new friends. He felt sufficiently relaxed to explain yet again to Catherine why she should not become pregnant until he had finished the PhD and got his first academic teaching post. Catherine listened in silence; for a long time she had known she did not want to become pregnant by him, but this was obviously not the assurance he wanted to hear. She said she understood, and changed the subject.

She and Mark were going to spend Christmas with his parents. She gritted her teeth and went. Elizabeth and Massimo were giving a party on New Year's Eve, and she focussed her mind on that. And on Demetrio, who would probably be there. Possibly.

She was tired and glad to be away from home. She slept a lot, used only half her mind, and found that Christmas was surprisingly bearable; Mark's parents seemed to have come to the conclusion that at least she was a known evil. Mark was happy because his work was still going well; they went for long walks in the sharp cold, drank in unreconstructed country pubs with roaring coal fires, and even kissed companionably under the mistletoe. It was nothing like real life, but it was a very pleasant interlude.

Back in the London flat, a phone message was waiting from Mrs Hughes Number Four: her mother had been taken to hospital three days before, after a heart attack. She refused Mark's offer to go with her, cancelled a dental appointment, left him to tell Elizabeth she would miss the party, and made for Euston. By the time the taxi dropped her off in the village it was dark. Mrs Hughes Number Four gave her a cup of strong tea and her mother's spare door-key.

It was strange to let herself into the familiar ice-cold house and know that the sharp familiar voice would not call out to her. She lit the fire so that the house would be warm in the morning and thought for a moment of using the spare bedroom where Mark always stayed, but the bareness of the room appalled her. In the end she took three hot-water bottles to the bed she had slept in since childhood.

'You needn't have bothered yourself to come,' said her mother, bright-eyed and cold the next morning. 'I'm doing very well here. Tell Mrs Davies Number Seven she might as well have come out to see the ambulance instead of watching through her curtains. And pay the milkman, but only for three pints.'

The doctors said it would take a week or more to finish

their tests. Catherine bought a week's supply of food in the supermarket and caught the bus back.

Her life fell into a new pattern: cleaning in the mornings, hospital in the afternoons, cooking in the evenings. She knew she should make contingency plans – domestic help for her mother? An old people's home? Should she get in touch with the distant cousins in Carmarthen? – but she was slothfully in limbo and could think of nothing.

On the sixth day, she returned from the hospital to see a car parked outside her mother's house which seemed so foreign that for a moment she did not recognise it. 'Happy New Year,' said Demetrio. He got out of the car and presented her with a bouquet of red and white carnations; he was grinning broadly.

She stood staring stupidly at him, aware that the net curtains at Number Seven were twitching avidly. She would have liked to ask him to leave immediately: two parts of her life could not be allowed to come together in this way. But he had come a long way in the cold and rain, had been waiting a long time for her to return, and was now shivering slightly in the dark of the dull winter afternoon.

'You'd better come in,' she said, thinking that this at least would remove him from Number Seven's view and realising only as the front door closed behind them that getting him into the house might be easier than getting him out.

He looked around the kitchen with interest. 'So this is where you come from?'

'No,' she said automatically, and then, 'Well, yes, but it's not me.'

He looked as if he was about to say something sarcastic, and then changed his mind. 'Do the flowers get water? They've been in their plastic paper long enough.'

Relieved at the change of subject, she filled a vase with

water. The kitchen seemed unnervingly smaller than usual. She started babbling, 'The flowers are so pretty – surely you didn't bring them all the way from London? And in the Welsh colours, too – how diplomatic!'

'Italian colours,' said Demetrio. 'Or Polish if you forget the leaves. And diplomatic I am not.'

She made coffee, and they sat looking at each other over the oilcloth-covered table.

Nothing, she thought, had prepared her for the least boring and predictable element in her life to appear without warning in the place where her life had been most boring and predictable. Her mind was full of questions: How did he know? Elizabeth? Had he got the address from Mark and, if so, how? How long had he been waiting for her to return? Did Mark know? *If he'd only go away and come back later I'd have time to think and get used to the idea of him being here, I could decide what I was going to do and have my reactions all planned before he came down the road. Asking him to leave now would be childish. And prudish. I'm a grown woman, and married, and I wish he'd go away so that I could think straight.*

'You could show me the house,' he said, picking up a holdall which seemed to have got from his car to the kitchen without human agency. And then, 'Yes, this one.'

'It's my mother's bedroom!'

'Your mother is not here, she doesn't need it. We, of course, do; it is the only double bed in the house. Which would be more comfortable. We are not little students, to spend the night falling off a single bed.'

Mother's bed! Unthinkable! The desecration!

I shouldn't have asked him in. I should have told him to go after the coffee. I know that to Mrs Davies Number Seven letting him into the house when my mother isn't here was an irretrievable sin that the whole village will hear about first thing tomorrow ('It's always the quiet ones are the worst. Reading all those old French books!') Mother, at the very latest, the day after (and probably the distant cousins in Carmarthen the day after that).

He had driven a long way in the cold and rain to see her and it was now dark, so he would have to stay: that was what adults did. And of course they would spend the night together, in her mother's double bed; that was also what adults did. If she was ever to break the bonds which kept her a child in that house, she might as well do it in style, outraging the neighbours and ruining the reputation her mother had so bitterly built for her over the years, with a man who belonged nowhere.

'Yes,' she said. 'Let us always be logical.' And smiled.

They went to bed early; there was, after all, nothing to wait up for.

She woke in the early hours of the morning; the room looked the same as it always had. He lay on her right side, his face in the pillow, his right arm across her. The rest of her body felt cold. She reached carefully to pull the sheet and blankets over them; he muttered something in his sleep but did not wake up. Mission accomplished, she thought. Whatever *that* was. The rain still beat heavily on the bedroom window, but she was warm in the battered, sagging old bed under the worn Welsh wool quilt.

She felt herself smiling, and could not stop. Her mind went back to a party in a French garden when she was fifteen, the discovery that she could get drunk on pleasure, the surprise of the world of new sensations, the mushrooms that had brought new tastes to her tongue.

And now, she thought, for the pastry.

THE COOK

~

Christine Hirst

'Of soup and love, soup is best.'

You read this out to me, smiling.

As if I didn't know. As if I wasn't that kind of cook. You think it isn't true, but I know better.

After all, that's how I seduce you, tempting you with little delicacies, at coffee time. And later, when you get to know me better, entertaining clients, with soups of every variety, hot or cold. Then, perhaps, a little asparagus served with hollandaise sauce and after that a steak covered in herb butter.

'Food to die for,' that's what Ken, your managing director, says as he has a second helping of my Sussex Pond pudding with lashings of thick cream. 'I should snap her up quick Richard, before someone else does.'

And so you do. And who could blame you? What I lack in looks I certainly make up for in the kitchen. But I always know, deep in the warmth of our soft bed, that it isn't me you dream about, when other appetites take over.

Daphne has gone now, Daphne of meals on wheels. I don't know her well because it's early days yet, but well enough to recognise her little mantras like 'Doing us proud again as usual' and 'Aren't we lucky' as she places the trays on the table. She implies that none of her other clients get such preferential treatment. I picture them making do with stale Spam sandwiches curling at the edges.

'There we are now, enjoy that, it'll certainly put roses in

our cheeks, won't it? Ta Ta for now and remember, we are what we eat.'

How could I forget? It's like scripture to me, the proper version. *Tell me what you eat and I'll tell you what you are.* These are the very words of that great French chef Anthelme Brillat Savarin, inscribed in the front of my favourite recipe book, the one I keep by the bed. Sometimes I think I hear you making a little joke about the pudding I've turned into, but she doesn't hear you. Daphne's version of my mantra leaves the way open for endless jokes. One day I'll show her the real thing.

I am sitting opposite you today. I'm in one of my quiet phases. You are smiling. It's a sunny day. There are roses beside you, just to add that little dimension of serenity. The sky is unusually blue even for summer. I struggle through Daphne's meal and sit for a while, watching the people passing by. Before too long I become aware of a growing sense of indigestion, of discomfort, which changes my mood. Gradually, imperceptibly, I become anxious and afraid. At these times my mind disconnects itself from the present, and lets the past come back to disturb me with all its buried fury.

Old people shouldn't have a history, shouldn't have suffered. Should never cry 'Why me?' We are old, unimportant, we have no voice; our role is clear and simple. Rejoice in the grandchildren, if not ours then those of others, and show eternal gratitude, to everyone, for everything.

The minutes pass. I am all nerves. I take the containers into the kitchen and try to settle down again, but it is no good. Something has changed, taken me back, to the place old people should never visit, the past.

It began the day I stayed off work with a bad cold.

I drift back to that one day, not wanting to, unable to do

otherwise. It's pouring with rain outside. The phone rings, I lean across the bed sniffing. I wipe my nose and pick up the receiver.

'Hello,' I say hoarsely.

'Is that Esther?'

'Yes,' I answer, not recognising the voice, desperate for a cup of tea before I have to talk to anyone.

'It's Wynn.'

'Wynn? Wynn who?'

'Wynn. You know. I work with Richard. He said you had a bad cold and were at home. Nothing too serious, is it?'

Wynn is one of those people who worry.

'Oh sorry, hello Wynn. No, just a cold. I'm a bit feverish. How is Mair?"

'She's well, and actually it was her who asked me to get in touch with you. You were so good about visiting her in hospital; she hasn't forgotten that. She insists I ring you about . . .'

His voice trails off. I sneeze.

'Oh Lord,' he says, 'this is more difficult than I thought it would be, but Mair said we owed it you in case of . . .'

I reach for a hankie and the paracetamol.

'Excuse me Wynn, I just need to blow my nose.'

I grasp the cup of tea, now cold and grey, and swallow two tablets. I wonder what it is. Redundancy?

'Sorry Wynn. What were you saying?'

'I feel I ought to warn you, or at least prepare you. It's Richard.'

I shiver.

'He's lost his job.'

'No no, nothing like that, it's, it's, oh God . . .'

'What?'

'He's been seen a lot with . . .'

Something starts to gnaw inside my stomach.

'Don't tell me it's another woman.'

'I was afraid you wouldn't believe me. Perhaps I shouldn't have rung.'

'Who?'

'Friend of your daughter's, I think.'

Deep inside, something knowing and ancient stirs and nods.

'How long?'

'Too long, and it's looking serious. God, I feel awful. Would you like Mair to . . .'

'No. No, I need time to think. Thanks. I'll ring off if you . . .'

I hang up.

It isn't true.

This is just a bad dream brought on by mixing too many patent medicines. It isn't true. Look at the photograph of the two of us, here, beside the bed. I take it, clutching at it, cradling it in my arms and holding it tight. Then, through my tears I look at it. The warmth in your eyes is unmistakable. It isn't true. Wynn is wrong. I press it hard against me, and the glass shatters in two against my breast.

When you phone a little later, so attentive and concerned, I tell you about the broken glass. Somehow it is important that you know.

'So sorry Richard, I must have knocked the photo over reaching for the water.'

I hear myself apologise. One half of me listens to the other, responding as you go on talking, two voices in one mind.

'You're not going out, are you? Oh, a client. Yes, I see. Dinner? No, don't disturb me if you're going to be late.'

I lie back exhausted.

Then it starts. In my fevered state, an argument between two voices in my head begins. *Look how his hours have become more and more erratic and his excuses odder.*

An ancient chorus of tired women filter into one.

Lots of men work late and go in on a Sunday. The voice of the wife, pleading. *Perhaps there's a big promotion on.*

He would have told you if there was.

Well, he is forgetful.

Not over a thing like that. He used to ask your advice, have people round for coffee and your shortbread. Networking, he called it. He was proud to be able to ask them home.

Well, he's more experienced now. He just keeps work at work.

He forgot your anniversary.

This hurts. The ancient woman knows it. I feel her sadness for me.

He had other things on his mind.

Yes?

Yes.

You never check up on him, do you?

Well, perhaps you should.

When he comes in looking flushed and tired I don't want to bother him.

Flushed? Tired?

All right.

At this I start to cry. But I knew. I have always known. I turn to my recipe book, beneath the inscription and the famous quotation I have written: 'Of soup and love, soup is the best'. Come what may, I will always be a good cook. This is my comfort. What claims can you make Richard, when you are overtaken by another rising star?

The next day you phone to say you'll be back early. You come home and kiss me. I have cooked cream of mushroom soup, lamb and green bean casserole and *crème brulée*. I watched the sugar melt, the little bubbles bursting and wondered at the clear glassy top, setting perfectly, as it cools. The excellent wine does its work. Everything is fond, normal.

We go to bed replete, happy. Yesterday recedes into a simple feverish dream.

I wake early, startled by a stream of sunlight, a throat of bird song in the garden like a greeting. Your mouth is already on mine. I feel you rolling down from me and then through a haze of sleepy happiness, five cold stabs tear the warm veiled air.

'I may move area, Esther.'

'Where to, Richard? I'll come with you.'

'No, you stay here. I'll come home weekends. It's a good move. But it's only for a short time.'

And then you shower, dress, eat the kedgeree I make for you and go, kissing me good bye.

'Only for a short time.' That light easy tone of yours, the hum of your car leaving.

My sleeping patterns grow disordered. I drift in a deep sadness. I sit, speculative, staring past the days, through the nights. They run together, all the colour bled away. The shock of the empty chair opposite, no one to touch to close the day.

No one to cook for. I go on unliving. Day follows day, life an improvisation. I pick at things, drink tea. There is no certainty without you. I go to bed alone.

At the weekend my kitchen is a sonata of fine sounds. Chopping, slicing, beating, whisking, blending; then it is all ready. I pour myself a drink and wait for the sound of your car. I wait and wait. I begin to lose all sense of time. You do not come. You do not ring. Your mobile phone is turned off.

On what I think is Monday I realise I should be back at work. I phone in sick again. This time they ask for a doctor's note. Good cooks are hard to find.

The next Friday there is a note through the post, written in haste. *'Home soonest. Can you cook for some clients, Friday night? Ken and his wife are coming. Ever yours, R.'*

I cook as I have never cooked before. Babette's feast. In

your absence I have lost half a stone. I can't cook if there is no one to please. But now I have a purpose. I decide to cook a galantine. Between the golden layers of aspic I place little rosettes from radishes, tomatoes and little curls of carrot, and fans of celery to complete its beauty. I play Bach's preludes and fugues, for what I need is accuracy, and then as the work progresses and my heart rides high, Vivaldi. I decorate the table with garlands of herbs, and in little clusters here and there I place baskets of spun sugar with raspberries inside, red as rubies. We begin with chilled apricot soup, and then I carry in the main course. It is greeted with rapturous applause. Then we enjoy the best of cheeses before the grand finale, Bombe Nesselrode.

The evening is an outstanding success, a symphony. Ken listens to his wife's remark that he will be digging his grave with his teeth, and refuses any offer of more. He looks at her and smiles. He loves her. I look at you. You do not love me. You use me to further your career. I give you more pudding. The ancient woman nods. After they have gone I say, 'Your Mother rang, she's a bit off colour, do you think you could pop over and see her sometime?'

'Of course,' you say, 'of course,' helping yourself to another brandy, 'tomorrow.'

Tomorrow is Saturday. Then you are already asleep in the chair.

The next day you are up, dressed and off before I'm awake. Later in the day I ring your Mother to see what time you will be back. You aren't there. Finally, I have to do it. I drive round to the flat that was once my daughter's and now belongs to Emily. Your car is parked outside. The ancient woman nods. I look in the mirror; there is hatred in my eyes. I plan a thing to which I cannot give a name.

Daphne arrives. She is resplendent in powder blue. She

is a big woman, statuesque, with shocking blond hair curled and whipped like a cream topping. When I admire her dress she says she has been to a colour consultant and it has changed her whole life.

'Avoid the beiges, dear. They're death to the skin, and black as well. I quarrel with it personally, and I'm pretty sure you would. Oh, here's a useful tip, save your reds until the autumn; they look much better then. It's to do with the leaves or something. Clever how they bring nature into it.'

She puts down the pre-cooked food and waves purple nails at the pudding.

'The wonders they can work with rhubarb! I just can't get over how inventive they can be.'

I peer closely beneath the custard, but the marvel remains hidden, like buried treasure. I make agreeable noises then as I look up Daphne sits down with a thump and bursts into tears.

'He's gone,' she says at last, red puffy eyes raised to mine. She blows her nose like a trumpet call. Daphne, twice divorced, deceived again. Her mascara runs in rivers.

'And I gave him such lovely dinners,' she sniffs. 'He'll never know the trouble I went to in choosing them. Those freezers are very deep you know, and the one you want is always at the bottom. But how could I compete with her? A stick of a girl half his age. You know the type. Salad all the time and colonic irrigation. And sex of course. It's not the same when you've got arthritis. Well, my heart's broke for good this time. If I hadn't had me colours done I wouldn't have been able to put up half the fight I have.'

Moved beyond words I get up out of my chair and cradle her head in my arms. She cries without restraint. I lend her my hankie, as hers is wet through. Soon we move on to the tissues. I hold her close. I am afraid to stroke the hair-do, so

I mutter, 'There, there,' and pat her shoulder. As I look down upon her head I notice that all her roots are grey.

'If he wants to leave,' I say, ' let him go. You'll soon find someone better to look after you.'

She looks at me and then across at you and appears thoughtful.

Then she makes a remark with such an air of finality something stirs and starts to shape up inside me.

'I've finished with men for good and that's the end of it.'

She kisses me on the cheek.

'You've been lovely to me, dear,' she says. 'It's a long time since I've known such kindness. Better make a move. The others will be expecting me.'

She sniffs and gathers herself up. 'It'll all be going cold now and I do pride myself on all my lunches being hot.'

And off she goes, leaving a trail of tissues and the exquisite delights of the rhubarb.

At 9.30 p.m. your mother rings.

'He has called in, dear. I asked him if he'd been playing golf and he said yes. He's on his way back now.'

I want it to be true. Still I want this against all the odds. His golf clubs are kept in the hall cupboard next to the phone. I see them as I pull open the door while she is speaking. I grow as hard as frost.

There are two photographs in the house of you on your own. I go into the dining room and take one up into my hand. One that I took a year ago. I look at it closely; I look at your eyes. Then I notice your gaze goes ever so slightly to the side of me. Who are you looking at? Is it me? Who else could it be? Then it comes back. My daughter and her boyfriend were standing beside me, Emily by my shoulder, watching, waiting. And then I know. That isn't the kind of loving look you direct at your son or daughter. It is too knowing. It is the look of a lover. I stare at it mesmerised and then it comes to me. He's on his way. Quickly I scrawl a note. *Terrible migraine. Gone to bed.*

And in the bedroom is that other photograph. The other one with tender knowing eyes. Who took that one? Emily.

In the morning I find a note. *Sorry you were ill, back at the weekend. Don't worry, R.*

I can't cook, but I make sure there is plenty in the fridge to prepare an appetising meal.

You come home at lunchtime on Saturday. Could I rustle something up for you? Short notice and all that, but you always were a sweetie. And your arm is round me, wooing me for your stomach. This is my chance. Food to die for. Casually over dinner I ask for a contact number. You seem surprised. Then you promise to leave your mobile phone turned on.

And so it begins. I become a weekend wife. I make a careful study of my menus. Butter, cream and eggs dominate my choices. Fats you won't know about, cooked in, added. I will welcome you with chocolate cake replete with half a pound of butter and six eggs. My delectable shortbread is smothered in creamy excesses. There is always plenty of brandy.

On and on I go, preparing menus like a thing possessed. Sauces thickened with eggs, and brandy butter always to hand. For several weekends things go beautifully. Then one weekend you do not come. An hour or so after the time that you usually arrive, I start to fret. I drive past all the restaurants you like. I drive for almost an hour. And then I see you going into one, hand in hand with Emily. She is young, beautiful and slim, in the skimpiest of dresses. Her underwear is evidently intended to be seen. I start to cry, but through my tears I can't help noticing that you have gained weight, that your waist band is a little tight, that you wear your jacket open. I hear the sound of ancient laughter.

During the week the cooker stands cold. But to keep myself busy I write cookery articles for magazines. Cook to grow slim, Cook to grow young, Food for love, Food for Success, Food to die for.

Gradually the weekends extend into Friday and Monday lunch times. Working from home you call it. You are getting a bit heavier and just a little breathless. One evening, fortified by brandy, I ask you if you have seen Emily lately. You peer at me over the top the newspaper you are reading, your glasses half way down your nose.

'Emily? Good Lord, haven't given her a thought for ages. No, I haven't seen her.'

We are so comfortable together and your voice is so mild that I almost believe you. At any rate I decide to let sleeping dogs lie.

When you are hanging up your jacket that night a photograph of you and her falls out of your pocket. The two of you together, your arm across her shoulder. I put it back and am sick in the bathroom. I can't bear it.

But photographs don't lie. I make myself look at it again. You were thinner then. The ancient woman smiles.

I flick through my old albums. They rewrite my history. Anyone would think I had spent my childhood endlessly playing by the sea and that all the days were sunny. No one snaps the gloomy November Sunday boredom, doing jig-saws as the rain comes down. So we forget about those days, the ones without pictures. I am always smiling in the snaps. You'd think I was a happy child. I wasn't. Far from it. We only use the camera for the days that stand out from the humdrum dreariness. But every now and then they show you something, something that wasn't meant to be seen. Like the old aunt all done up in her Sunday best, smiling with her lips closed. A lovely face. But something wrong about the mouth. I stare at it for ages and then it hits me, she hasn't got any teeth and is trying to hide it. And then of course, there are the ones that show the direction of your smile. No one will ever know the truth about you and me. Truth can only be uncovered in diaries or letters. I never write anything down. There are no photographs of us together in all these years.

In the end she asks you to go and you come back to me. The best part of my married life has gone to her. But she now has someone new, younger. We grow older together, and during all those years I ask no questions, playing the dutiful wife. I give my full attention to your welfare. I fetch and carry for you. I spare you any worries. I encourage you to drink with old colleagues.

'I'll pick you up, darling. Then you don't have to worry about how much you have.'

You don't go out much. One evening you come home from golf complaining of chest pain. I pour a large brandy and give it to you with two paracetamols. You go to bed and in the night you suffer a massive heart attack. I am a little late calling the doctor. There is nothing he can do. Now all that's left of you is the photograph I keep beside your chair. How well I play the grieving widow.

After the funeral the doctor alerts Social Services that I am losing weight and will not cook for myself. I am reluctant to leave my bed and am becoming a bit frail. And so they send in carers to get me up. There is nothing wrong with me. I just can't cook. Really, I'm quite fit.

I decide to give myself a holiday. I flick through the magazines I used to write for, which also advertise culinary courses. And brochures for the over sixties, still young at heart. I could go abroad and learn to cook exotic dishes in the sun. Perhaps I'll try India. All those glorious spices. I could learn to cook over a real fire in the open air. But first of all I need someone to cook for. That is the problem. Who could there be? I think and think. The children both live abroad now. I have no friends or relatives I could call on. It seems hopeless. I almost give up on the idea.

But then suddenly I see a movement in the window, a car, a face. Daphne! I smile broadly. I am overjoyed. Anyone watching would think it was your photograph at which I am smiling so fondly. But they would be quite wrong. My gaze falls just a little to the left of you. A tiny clue that my life has changed forever. Not that you'd notice in the normal run of things.

BRONWERDD

~

Imogen Rhia Herrad

I think I may have made a mistake.

She is looking at me oddly, and she has been asking me some strange questions.

Maybe it would have been better if I hadn't done it, I can see that; but there's not much I can do now.

She's gone out. I don't know where she is. The house is chilly and silent.

I don't think I knew what I was doing at the time and I wouldn't have ever thought that it would come off. I think I must have been a bit drunk, on the wine and the summer heat and the moon.

I'd been longing for a companion. Well, not *longing*. Wishing. I think the move unsettled me, and the new job. Being made head chef, just like that, when I'd never expected it. In that big old castle too – somebody told me the foundations went right back to the Middle Ages. And the cellars. The wine cellar.

That's what started it, those old bottles of wine. I know wine couldn't really be that old, but I wonder about those dusty bottles we found right at the back. When I went home that night I took one of them with me, just to taste.

Perhaps there was something in it beside wine, something that came out when I opened it, something that came over me.

I've never felt as strange as I did after that first glass.

I'd been in the kitchen all day long, with the heat and the

steam and all the smells of herbs and vegetables cooking; and I had just one glass before going home. All night long I dreamt, of juicy leaves and succulent greens, so many shades of green. The piercing smell of rosemary, the sweet stinging scent of lavender, and above all the dark, green fragrance of spinach.

I woke up with spinach on my brain. I woke up and saw green. I could not get spinach out of my mind.

I was like this for a week. Obsessed. Its iron taste on my tongue, its bitter scent in my nostrils.

I fell in love with spinach.

It was perhaps in the nature of this love that it was unrequited, but I could not accept that. There must be something, I thought, something I can do.

I wanted consummation, not consumption.

I dreamt again that night and when I woke up, with the moon shining right into my eyes, so bright that for a moment I thought it was the sun and time to get up, I had an idea. I got up and went down to the kitchen like a sleepwalker – but I was wide awake – and I got that bottle of wine out, which wasn't maybe such a good idea.

There was spinach growing in the vegetable garden. I pulled up a lot of that, and a couple of lettuces for lightness and strawberries for sweetness.

I made myself a fair maiden, out of vegetables and fruit, not flowers. I made a spinach woman to be my friend and my companion and my only love.

I gave her wine for blood and lemon juice for zest. Lavender for longing, sage for wisdom and also bitterness. Cinnamon, ginger and saffron for dreams and mystery, olive oil for depth, and a pinch of salt because without salt life would have no taste.

I gave her rose petals for lips and black cherries for her eyes; and I named her Bronwerdd, because her skin when she came alive in the moonlight was as green as grass, as green as spinach, and she was beautiful beyond my dreams.

For many weeks I was happy. I wanted nothing more than her tender fingers, her tendril fingers, curled round mine; the taste of her green green skin, her rose petal mouth, on my lips.

I was content.

But now things have changed. She has changed.

She does not like me eating vegetables; she calls me a cannibal. She has taken to reading the *Encyclopedia Britannica*. I have not dared tell her that I am a chef in a vegetarian restaurant. She insists that I keep a non-vegetable diet. When I tried to explain that I am a vegetarian because I do not like eating living things, she went dark green with anger and said, 'Are plants not living things then? I'm alive, aren't I?'

I think it better, for the time being, to eat eggs and cheese when I'm in the house and have all other meals at work.

The country frightens her, because although there is a lot of plant life there, she is afraid of the sheep and the cows and refuses to come hill-walking with me.

'Come on,' I said the first time we went. 'They're not going to eat you.'

I wasn't thinking.

She gives me odd looks, and she spends a lot of time sitting in the garden, sifting soil through her fingers and toes.

A couple of weeks ago she got drunk on plant food and refused to come in for the night.

She is giving me powders to take with a glass of water every day. They are to grow me out of my cannibalistic habits, she says. She makes them out of minerals and ground stones. They taste very strange.

I have begun to feel funny, these last few days.

The day before yesterday I caught her kissing the rosemary bush.

She pretended she had only been smelling it, turned away immediately and started to talk about the weather. She said she was hoping for rain; it had been dry for so long and she was drooping.

At work, I made a huge bowl of leaf salad and ate it all.

I felt very sick afterwards.

I looked positively green in the mirror.

Maybe I have made a mistake. Perhaps we are not suited.

But then I think of her eyes and her rose red lips and the sweet, bitter taste of her skin, and everything else melts away.

When I came home yesterday there was the smell of rosemary all over her.

She had a glass of plant food on the rocks in her hand, and offered me one too.

'No, thank you,' I said. 'I don't think it would do me much good.'

'Are you sure?' She watched me. 'Do you think it would poison you?'

'Probably.'

She wanted to know what dosage might kill me.

'That glassful might do it,' I said, pouring myself a glass of white wine. She has only got to the letter R in the *Encyclopedia Britannica* and hasn't found out yet that wine is a vegetable product.

I have been home from work for over two hours now. I have just taken the last of her powders, and it is making me feel most peculiar.

The wine tastes odd too.

She has gone out. I don't know where she is. The house is chilly and silent without her.

There is a patch of newly dug, dark, moist soil in the garden. The air is filled with the heady scent of fresh earth. I am feeling very tired; my feet are sore and dry. It strikes me that this cool, damp soil would feel wonderful against my skin. So I take off my shoes and dig my feet into the ground.

This is heaven.

I had no idea the earth felt so good.

So like home.

THE GO-GO MAN

~

Gail Hughes

Of all my mother's lovers, who were many and varied during the years my sister and I were growing up, the go-go man is the one I shall never forget. He was the crowning glory of a collection of truly abysmal men, at least as far as Stella and I were concerned, and we're experts. After all, we were the ones who had to bear the brunt of our mother's amorous activities.

We called him the go-go man because he always seemed to be on the run. You could tell that his mind was racing ahead to the next thing on the agenda. His real name was Jack Busby. He was a large man with a receding hairline and bushy eyebrows that masked the worry lines on his face, and gave him the look of a friendly dancing bear. He wasn't exactly handsome, but there was something comfortable about him.

He was entirely unlike Giorgio, our mother's previous lover, who was small, thin and narcotically challenged. He'd fallen so passionately for her in the B'wise on Palace Street that he abandoned his return coach to Cremona, Italy, and threw himself on her mercy. After the usual period of revelry, our mother ejected Giorgio from her bed, but he would not go.

He remained, penniless, on our sofa, glowering at anyone foolish enough to enter the room. It was our sitting room, after all, so obviously this state of affairs could not continue. Our mother was forced to stop feeding him. But even a week of nothing but cold baked beans didn't budge him. So she turned off the hot water, which was the final straw for poor Giorgio who was very fond of his morning shower. He pranced down the road to the office of Mr Jones, the solicitor, who lent him the fare back to Italy.

Our mother was a generous woman at heart. As she saw him smoothing his hair in front of our mirror for the last time, she relented.

'I'm sorry, Giorgio, that it's ended like this.'

'No, you are not,' he hissed. Then he flounced out of our house forever.

It's true that none of the men in Lavinia's life seemed to last very long. Not even our father. She left him on a lay-by in France shortly before Stella was born, or so the story goes. But when I think of Lavinia nowadays, I realise it was because she had too much love inside her. She wanted to embrace the whole world. How could she settle for one mere specimen of a single sex? The fact that she ended up on her own with two children in a tatty house opposite a paint factory was nothing short of tragic. Because she was beautiful.

By the time the go-go man took up residence in our mother's bed – for even though he was seldom there, the letters and phone calls seemed to confirm his presence – we were all in need of some equilibrium. The beginning was magnificent: it really did seem as though our family had made it into some kind of normal existence at last.

There were fresh peaches and cream cakes and cut flowers in the vases when the go-go man came to call. Everything in the house became cleaner and finer. Our grandmother's white curtains, which had languished for years in boxes, appeared at the windows, bright and billowing, and the bathroom was suddenly spotless. Our mother stopped baking the hard indigestible loaves she had forced down us since infancy; instead, we found white sliced bread on the table and little pots of jam.

For days after each one of the go-go man's visits a magic aura prevailed. Lavinia would wander about the house, humming, oblivious of anything Stella and I might be up to. She would press chocolates into our palms and urge us to settle in front of the telly so she could pursue her reverie. Until the go-go man's arrival upon the scene our mother had worn her heart on her sleeve, joking that she'd left her chastity belt back in the dark ages, by which she meant the fifties. But after she met Jack Busby, Lavinia put away her leotards, her Indian cottons and hippie beads. She began to act like an adult.

It's only now, since my friends have married and even Stella has a husband and children that I begin to dwell on relations between the sexes. When I observe that war zone called family life, I realise how lonely and frustrated Lavinia must have been. But, quite frankly, I cannot imagine a worse fate than being locked in married combat with a man. It could be I haven't the temperament for it either. Aside from a brief encounter for the purpose of losing my virginity, the sort Lavinia would have approved of, I've kept pretty much to myself. I used to be afraid I'd end up on the shelf.

But I'm getting ahead of myself. It's the go-go man I was telling you about.

We found him in Gerrard's tea-room, a place we did not normally frequent. I was nine and Stella was six at the time. It was the first day of the summer holidays and Lavinia had parked our old mini in front of the post office and accidentally dropped the keys down a drain. When we returned with armloads of shopping, only to find ourselves locked out, Lavinia dragged me and Stella, blubbering and quarrelling, to the nearest cafe in order to regroup and decide what to do.

While she was ordering tea, complaining to the cashier and flinging her long blonde hair from side to side in exasperation, a man, who was devouring a large plate of chips at one of the front tables, watched us. When Lavinia plonked our tray down on a nearby table, the man turned and said, 'Excuse me, ma'am, but I couldn't help hearing you tell the cashier about your keys. If it would help you at all, I could run you home with the children.'

'Thank you very much, but there's a bus at half past three.'

'Right you are, I was only trying to help,' and he turned back to his *Daily Mail*.

Lavinia must have had second thoughts because after a moment she said, 'Hello? You wouldn't happen to have a pen, would you? So I could leave a note on the car for the traffic warden.'

'Certainly do,' he said, groping in the inside pocket of his jacket for a silver Parker, 'I'm Jack Busby.'

'Just call me Vinny,' said our mother with a smile.

After Giorgio, it seemed almost too good to be true. The gogo man carried mint humbugs in the pockets of his baggy trousers. He had an almost inexhaustible supply of elephant jokes, and gaudy ties, which we used to tie his wrists together, and he let Stella and I raise and lower the electric windows of his long grey car, up and down, faster and faster, until we collapsed in hysterics on the back seats, which smelled of polish and leather.

There were no more passionate slanging matches in the kitchen; instead, dinners in cafes for all four of us. No slamming of doors, just murmurs from the bedroom. And not only was the go-go man negligent with the 50p coins that rolled beneath our sofa – he had an income. He was the sales rep for a paper towel company based in Swansea and he also moonlighted for a private health scheme. In fact he had his finger in so many pies that in time it became difficult to know whether Lavinia was his sugar plum fairy or just a bit of left-over pastry that had almost reached its sell-by date. But in the beginning, we were entranced.

It's strange how these memories illuminate the present. Like iridescent balls on a Christmas tree, they twist and shine, and the smallest things – a lavender hair ribbon, the sort Lavinia used to wear, a flash of pink plastic sandal, a golden buttercup beside the road – they all send me along the pathways to Lavinia. Whether these colours gleam so brightly because of the sea mists, or the sombre greyness of this town, I cannot say.

Looking back, I can see that Jack Busby was the first proper adult our mother ever had. All the rest were children: jesters, musicians, gay-boys. Except for Mel the Turk who worked at the paint factory across the road and came by on Thursday evenings with a bottle of wine, they simply wanted to crawl in under Lavinia's skirts where there was not enough room for us all.

But the go-go man ushered in an era of romance. Whenever he passed through, we were always his first stop. When he was not actually in residence, we waited; Lavinia, wringing her hands, for a phone call to put her out of her misery; Stella and I, for the mood of the house to be lifted by the promise of a firm date, a gesture of redemption.

At first he came in the afternoons while Stella and I were in school, but later it was for whole nights. Once he took us in his car to the seaside where he bought us buckets and spades and an inflatable plastic duck and Stella and I went mad with excitement while he and Lavinia wandered along the beach, hand in hand. At Christmas, he did not come at all, but a delivery van brought a single red rose in a sealed plastic bubble that lasted into January when Stella and I went back to school. Sometime that spring Lavinia began to wear a ring.

Spontaneity had always been our mother's religion. She was lithe and vivacious and she gave the impression that her life was an accidental orgasm of truth and light. Much as she loved me and Stella, we had often felt like leg irons, holding her back from glory. But the go-go man changed all that: she became softer, calmer, maternal almost. When he wasn't there she seemed content to dream by the window. We had to acknowledge his magic, and some of it must have rubbed off on us as well because we let him take liberties that none of the others were allowed. There was always a box of chocolates or some new game for Stella and I, so we were able to be magnanimous.

With hindsight, I can see it was inevitable that one day Lavinia should have been walking, hand in hand with Stella and I, along a row of lion's cages in Chester Zoo and that she should have looked up and seen Jack Busby in front of the golden puma, flanked by a mousy lady with pink lipstick and canvas shoes and a small boy with a face like a squashed tomato. It was the boy who surprised us most. He was just a bit younger than Stella and was jumping up and down, crying, 'Dad! Dad! I wanna see the orang-utan. I wanna see him NOW.'

Stella's face lit up when she saw the go-go man. She started towards him, but then she saw the cold clutch of fear in Lavinia's eyes and froze in her tracks. Jack Busby gave a small shrug of recognition. Then he turned to the boy.

'C'mon, Orlando. Daddy will take you straightaway.' And he set off at a trot, or you might say a gallop, with the mouse-woman cantering along behind him.

Lavinia was devastated. She didn't say a word as we walked through the rest of the zoo. She brought us home, cooked tea and sat opposite us at the kitchen table. But she didn't eat or talk, either that day or the next, when a huge bouquet of chrysanthemums arrived. Lavinia placed them on the window sill, and threw the card in the fire.

The following day, an envelope in Jack Busby's sloping hand plopped through the letter slot while Lavinia was still in bed. She tore it open, glanced at the letter with a severe expression and tossed it aside, but when Stella and I deciphered it later, we knew she was going to forgive him.

'My darling Vinny, I did not know how to tell you. But things are not as they seem. My marriage has been . . .' and here a word was scratched out but we finally made out 'mori-bund', then some more scratching and then, 'My wife begs me to stay so I am here, for the time being. I dream of the day when you and I will be together. I love you always. Your Jack.'

After the letter, Lavinia cheered up a bit but she still looked drab and thin. She had taken to wearing greys and mauves, and a silky pastel shawl with silver threads, a present from the go-go man. Sometimes the pallor of her skin was indistinguishable from her clothing.

The amazing thing was, before long, the go-go man was back in Lavinia's bed. At first things seemed a bit odd but after a while they returned to normal. The go-go man spent just as long lovingly closeted in our mother's bedroom as he had before each departure. The mouse woman and the little boy Orlando didn't seem to matter any more, though in our hearts, Stella and I were not convinced and I don't think Lavinia was either. But we all pretended. We had grown dependent on the go-go man, on the treats and the outings. We had to have him, to make our lives worth living.

It seems to me now, that if Lavinia had only had the strength to send the go-go man packing things might have been okay. We could have gone back to our jesters and brother buddies, and Mel from the paint factory would surely have come calling once again. But you see, none of us wanted change. We simply couldn't leave the go-go man alone.

I don't know why my thoughts are constantly with Lavinia. It's now five years since she went to the hospital. I know she is far happier in the house where she now lives than she was for a long time. There were too many memories around our old kitchen table. Things which couldn't be aired away, things which grew more dense and oppressive as time went by. These days Lavinia is constantly surrounded by people, which is what she always wanted. If some of them are strange or mad, they're friendly enough. So why is she on my mind?

I find myself thinking of our last outing with the go-go man, the day we went to Carlo's Ice Cream Parlour down by the bus depot. He had not taken us out *en famille* for some time. I suppose it might have been predicted that once he'd wormed his way back into Lavinia's favour with chrysanthemums and After Eights, his visits would grow shorter and less frequent. They were now often mid-week, which meant that Stella and I were excluded. On the few occasions when we saw him as we arrived home from school, he was on his way out the door.

But one Saturday, he arrived at midday in an ebullient mood and hustled us out to his car, despite Lavinia's protests about soup cooking. Once we got to Carlo's, the go-go man waved the luncheon menu aside and whispered something into the Corsican waiter's ear. Then he said something in broken Italian to Carlo, who was behind the cash desk, sorting through a pile of CDs. Carlo beamed and put on Frank Sinatra. The music came blaring through the loud-speakers as he strolled over to our table, bent over Lavinia's blonde head, gave her a noisy kiss on the cheek, and said, 'Thisa funnyman, Jack Busby. Very good friend. I dunno what I do without him.'

Then Carlo placed a brown paper packet on the table in front of the go-go man. It looked as though it might contain several CDs. I can remember wondering if they were for Stella and I, or whether he was going to keep them for Orlando.

The waiter arrived with huge oval dishes of different flavours of ice cream, sprinkled with chopped nuts and candied fruit, and topped with chocolate sauce and whipped cream. He set them down in front of Stella and I.

Jack Busby picked up the packet and popped it in Lavinia's bag.

'Can you keep this till we get to the car?' he asked. The waiter returned with three scoops of chocolate for him, and for Lavinia a half pineapple, stuffed with chopped straw-berries and cream, and big glasses of coke for us all.

A festive atmosphere prevailed, though none of us had any idea why. The go-go man laughed and joked until the customary anxious look, which Lavinia had worn of late, fell away and she began to look quite radiant. Stella and I sat silently, ploughing our way through the ice cream, but the bowls were enormous and, after a while, we began to get annoyed. It was all very well, this stuffing of our faces, keeping us quiet while he and Lavinia carried on as though we weren't there. But I for one was beginning to realise that the ice cream was nothing more than a cheap bribe.

I don't know why it was that Stella and I decided, at the same moment and quite independently, to pierce their bubble. Stella began by striking her spoon against her empty glass like an after dinner speaker at a wedding.

'Ladies and gentleman,' she tittered, clinking in time to the syllables. I joined in the tapping, adding a hollow thunk to Stella's resonant bell. The go-go man was in the midst of telling Lavinia an involved story about the boss of the private health scheme, gripping her with his brown trout eyes so that she was unable to tear her attention away from him, even though she knew trouble was brewing. All she could do was make a gesture across the table, which we, of course, ignored.

Stella grabbed the amaretto wafer from her ice cream and began to feed me, while I made seal noises. Then she grabbed my wafer and I grunted and snuffled and tried to bite her hand. And so she lobbed a huge splodge of ice cream towards me, but it missed my mouth and fell onto the tablecloth. In retaliation, I took my spoon and levered my last remaining scoop, dripping with chocolate sauce, from the bowl. And as Frank Sinatra crooned away in the background I launched it at Stella but it flew wide of the mark. We watched, fascinated, as the gooey blob landed smack in the middle of the go-go man's forehead.

He went absolutely silent. So did Stella and I.

The ice cream began to dribble down over his eyebrows and along the bridge of his nose. It seemed to take forever to reach the tip. Then it started to drip down onto his white shirtfront. We shrank from Lavinia's look of frozen embarrassment, realising that everyone's eyes were focused on our table.

A hush of horror hung over the Ice Cream Parlour.

Then Carlo was at our table, mopping the go-go man's brow and slapping him on the back and chanting in his sing-song voice things like, 'Children will be children.' What happened after that I don't really remember, only Lavinia's fury when the go-go man finally deposited us in front of our house that afternoon, having first made a detour to drop the parcel hidden in her bag through the letter slot of a house on the outskirts of town. That was the beginning of the end.

Lavinia was never the same after the day Jack Busby left forever. I remember when Stella and I came home from school; he was there, in the sitting room, though his car wasn't parked outside. We could hear his voice as we opened the door, so we crept along the passageway until we could see into the room without ourselves being seen.

'Lavinia, it's a job. I have no choice,' he was saying, hands spread, palms wide open and empty, eyes rolling to the heavens. We heard Lavinia's sharp intake of breath.

'When are you going?'

'Today. On the 5.13 to Manchester. My luggage is at the station. I just had to see you before I left.'

'So what do I do?' said Lavinia, in a small hopeless voice.

'Join me, Vinny! Come out to Africa and join me and we'll start a new life together, us and the girls. Start anew!'

He clasped her hands and stared into her eyes until Stella and I had to sneak away along the passageway to avoid laughing.

The go-go man kissed Lavinia and then left her blinking, defenceless in the doorway. It was only afterwards, when she wandered back into the sitting room with a mug of tea, that she noticed the brown case containing his sunglasses on the coffee table. The clock said twenty to five.

'I must go' she cried, grabbing the case. 'I have to give these to Jack! Watch telly. I'll be back.'

'No, Mummy,' I cried. 'I'm coming with you.'

'And me,' chimed Stella. So the three of us ended up running the half-mile to the railway station. We arrived just before five, but the platform was empty.

'There was a train to Crewe at 3.50,' the conductor said, looking sympathetically at Lavinia, who was clutching the glasses case in one hand and her shawl in the other. 'He may have been on that one.'

'Surely not,' our mother cried. She flew along the platform like a wounded bird, searching each bench, each alcove, dipping into the cafe and the waiting rooms, hovering near the door of the men's loo until the 5.13 had come and gone and it was obvious that no-one was lurking inside.

Instead of buoying her up, Jack Busby had drained the life out of her. He had stolen her sparkle.

The pearly evening folded around us. Lavinia began to cry. Stella and I didn't know what to do so we said, 'C'mon mum, we'll get some chips on the way home.'

And that was the end of the go-go man. Nobody ever saw him again.

After the go-go man's departure, Lavinia went into decline. She became even thinner and took to languishing on the sofa where Giorgio had slept and where she had kissed the go-go man for the last time. She would sit, hugging her knees, and rocking back and forth as though sheer concentration might bring him back again. Sometimes she listened to the Chopin tape he had given her.

One day there was a knock upon the door and there was a policeman.

'Jack Busby, madam,' he said, 'I believe you are acquainted with him.'

Lavinia turned pale.

'No, no,' she said.

'I don't suppose you'd be knowing his whereabouts, would you madam?'

'No,' said Lavinia.

'It's a matter of some urgency,' said the policeman, 'relating to some stolen property. We have information that he might contact you.'

'Oh, no,' gasped Lavinia.

'Well, madam,' said the policeman, 'I'll leave my card in case you hear anything. May I remind you that it's a criminal offence to obstruct a police investigation.'

And that was that.

The paint is peeling from the walls but this doesn't bother me. The plaster's rosy hue reminds me of summer days, of happier times, when we were all together. I sit in my room, thinking of Lavinia.

COQUETTE AU CAFÉ

~

Christine Harrison

Reaching out, she touched him ever so lightly on the arm.

'It's you,' she said.

She felt that, if she let him pass by, she would never see him again.

Her fingers blindly searched her purse. The flower-seller was wrapping mimosa in cellophane.

'Just a minute. I must pay for my flowers. What are you doing here?' There was a dark, unsteady jump in her voice.

'Paying for your flowers,' he said.

'Yes, thanks. Thanks.' Paying for her flowers was not the same as buying her flowers.

He should have walked on, he supposed, but it was too late. Especially as, in reaching over with the money, his hand accidentally touched her wrist. He had not seen her for six years.

'I always buy the first mimosas I set my eyes on,' she said.

They stood there on the pavement, not really knowing what came next. There was a faint impatience between them, whether to go or linger.

'I had one or two things to do up here,' he said. They began walking slowly away from the High Street and turned into an alleyway which was quieter, where they could think what to do, after six years.

The alleyway, with its small shops, was darker as well as quieter. They passed the second-hand bookshop and a couple of antique shops, their pace becoming even slower. Someone suddenly switched on a light in the window of the French pâtisserie, one bright window in the gathering dusk in that dim alleyway. The shops on either side had already closed early this winter's afternoon.

But the pâtisserie was lit up. It was a window of perfection. All the little cakes sitting there in their frilly paper cases, all so different, so tempting, so seductive with their glamorous icings and pretty decorations, waiting there in the window.

'There's a room in the back,' she said. 'Let's go in.' She laughed at his look of alarm. 'It's a sort of tea-room,' she said. 'Let's have a cup of tea.'

She meant, Let me lick out an éclair, light as air. Let me taste an orangy madeleine or one of those chocolaty things. '*Come buy. Come buy,*' her thoughts tried to whisper in his ear. He pushed the door open for her. It made a silvery bell ring. Elfin bell. Goblin bell.

But there was a screen across the little tea-room.

'It's closed, madam,' said the woman behind the counter, 'and we're closing soon.'

Her face was closed too, a 'seen it all before' sort of face. There was a notice on the folding screen saying 'Tea-Shop Closed'. The notice was pinned on, a last minute thought; a sign saying, Not this way, not here. Somewhere else perhaps. Go up to the end of the alleyway, turn right.

'Let's take a cake home,' she said suddenly, not looking at him as she spoke. 'We'll have a pot of tea and just one cake each. Only one, mind.'

She had a funny strict look – he remembered it.

She shifted her flowers onto her other arm, her coat falling back from her wrist. The yellow flowers and green leaves inside the crackling cellophane as under a skin of ice.

'I must leave you now,' he said, 'or I shall be late.'

Their eyes met at last.

'Oh well, it doesn't matter that much,' he sighed. 'It can wait.'

She smiled. 'Choose your cake,' she said. 'What about one of those apricot things? Or frangipane? You like almonds. I do remember that.'

But there were so many little cakes. How to choose just one? The cake tongs in the woman's hand hovered over the scallop-shelled madeleines, élcairs, cigarette russes with ends dipped in chocolate and chopped pistachios, the pretty tartelettes aux fruits with their glazed black and white grapes, wild strawberries, cherries and loganberries, and all the other sweet little tempting things. All of them only waiting to be gobbled up.

'Oh look,' she said, addressing the woman, '*they* look delicious. What are they called?'

'Coquettes au café,' said the woman, suppressing a yawn. The tiny cakes were two coffee-coloured rounds of meringue stuck together and half concealing a crystallized cherry.

'My mouth waters just to look at them,' she told him. '*Figs to fill your mouth. Citrons from the south. Cakes for dainty mouths to eat. Come buy. Come buy.*' This sang in her head so loudly she wondered he could not hear.

'Have you chosen?' she asked him. 'Oh yes, that one looks very delectable, and a little bigger than the rest perhaps, and I'll have the coquette thing.' She fished for her purse. 'No, I'll get these.'

Placed with practiced delicate care in their white box, the two cakes looked glamorous but lonely, just the two of them separated by tissue. The woman folded the box lid over them and tied thin paper ribbon around in an expert strangling movement, finishing with a loop for carrying the box.

As they went out of the shop to the sound of the tinkling bell, the woman at once began taking trays of cakes out of the window and switching off lights.

In the alleyway, hailstones, frozen from a shower earlier that day, still lay in the gutter. There was a certain cold nostalgic smell that he knew. The hailstones and the light in the pâtisserie suddenly going out, and then the way she carried her flowers; he knew he would not be able to forget. But especially the way she carried her flowers.

Women carry flowers when they marry. They also carry flowers to loved ones' graves. She was not doing either of these things. She was just walking through the darkening alleyway towards the house which used to be their home where she still lived, now in its basement flat. She held her head high as she walked.

They could see their breath in the air when they spoke.

'I suppose a cup of tea would be nice,' he said. He carried the cakes carefully not trusting the loop.

'Of course it would,' she said. 'And your cake. Your coquette au café.'

'That was the one you chose, my dear.'

'That's right, it was. Yours was the other thing.'

He used to call her darling, my darling. What did 'my dear' mean? they both wondered. It meant something, but it was not clear what.

He dreaded the house.

And hesitated as she led him down steps to the basement kitchen.

'You'll break your neck one day on these steps. Why don't you get rid of the moss?'

'I like it.'

'It's dangerous.'

'Mm.' She fished out her key, switching on the outside light for him. She opened the door. The kitchen smelled of oranges. There was a bag of them on the kitchen table and they had spilled out onto the moss-green chenille cloth.

'It' s like your burrow down here,' he said.

'I know. I love it. I would die if I had to leave it.'

He had thought she might die when he left her, but she did not. In a way it had been he who had partly died especially after his affair was over. She had just tunnelled into this dark place which she lit up with bright fabrics and bunches of flowers.

She took the cake box and cut the ribbon. She placed the two cakes on a fluted white plate and set them in the middle of the table. She took the oranges out of the bag and put them in the bowl in the window. She put on the kettle and found napkins, silver spoons, cups and saucers, a knife and cake forks.

'Cake forks,' he sneered, in his old sarcastic way.

He did not look at her, but only sensed her movements about the room as she arranged her flowers in a graceful glass jug which she placed in a dim corner. He felt, though he repressed it as best he could, that he might fall into a panic and do something extreme. Walk out without a word. Strangle her. He sat very still, his hands on his knees hidden under the table, and looked at the cakes in their frilly cases.

She poured boiling water into the tea-pot and the fragrance of tea-leaves floated up and mingled with the smell of oranges.'

'No milk,' he said, clearing his throat.

'I remember that. Of course I do.'

'I've changed you know. So much has changed. *I* have changed.

She passed him a cup of tea in the silence that followed. Everything in the room was silent, listening for what else he might say, for what his words might mean. He sipped his tea and took his cake, the tartelette aux fruits.

She smoothed the tablecloth. 'I saw Rose the other day,' she said.

About to bite into the cake, he stopped and put it down again.

'Oh Rose, I haven't seen her for ages. She's been in Germany, I believe. We lost touch.'

It was as if Rose had never meant anything to him. It was as if losing touch with Rose was nothing.

He bit into his cake.

He scooped a wild strawberry out of it with his tea-spoon and inspected it as if it might be an unknown insect.

'It's just a wild strawberry. Isn't it perfectly pretty? So perfect. *We must not buy their fruits. Who knows upon what soil they fed? Their hungry thirsty roots.*' Her thoughts sang their warning.

'Delicious,' he said as he bit into the rest of his cake. He licked his lower lip, and picked up the crumbs with a wetted finger.

'Good.'

'It was very sweet.'

There was some sweetness left. If he went. she might never see him again in this life. She might live to be seventy, eighty, even longer and never see him again. She would see thousands and thousands of other people in all those years but never him. She still had the key of the door in her pocket. How could she keep him, make him her prisoner?

'I wonder why our paths crossed today,' she said pouring more tea. 'The whole of London and our paths crossed. More tea?'

'Could I have a glass of water? It's made me thirsty. I'm not used to sweet things. Never eat cakes these days. And that was intensely sweet.'

'But you enjoyed it.' She crossed the room and went out into the kitchen to get some water. The kitchen window looked over a garden full of ferns.

'After, all that, she goes off to Germany,' she said over the sound of running water.

In her mind's eye she saw the English channel swallowing ferry boats one after another, and all the people drowning or swimming for their lives. She saw aeroplanes falling from the sky.

'I believe that's where she went.' He wiped his mouth with the napkin. 'But now she's back, you say.' He reached out for the glass of water.

'Yes, she's back.'

Something flickered across his face and she watched as it passed over his features. Something had absorbed his thoughts. She wanted to throw the water over him. Attack him with her cake fork.

'Drink up,' she said, 'if my cake has made you thirsty.'

'Where did you see her?'

'Another coincidence. At the Exhibition.' She laughed at this.

'Oh, the Icons Exhibition.'

'How did you guess?'

'She always liked that sort of thing, you know. Churchy things. I meant to go. I missed it.'

'If you had . . .'

'I heard it was very good.' He coughed. He was imagining her, she knew, in the flickering light of the candles against the gold of the icons. She knew his very thoughts. She read them.

'Yes, churchy thing,' she agreed. 'She was wearing something. A crucifix set with garnets or perhaps rubies. It looked expensive.'

'It wasn't all that expensive.'

'No? It looked it.' Her laugh this time was merrily incredulous.

'Not really. Junk jewellery.'

'No, not junk I think. But just tell me one thing.'

'I must go,' he said, half rising.

But it was as if fairy threads held him and made him sink back again into his chair. He became afraid. He was afraid of her lovely white wrists, her placid brow and the sweetness of her cakes and her fleeting expressions, He was afraid too, of the power and strength of her memories, her thoughts, her hidden emotions, the things that were unsaid between them. Rose had told him, 'You are afraid of her at bottom, why is that?' He did not know. Perhaps she was his conscience. There was no doubt that they should never have parted. It was an unnatural act, it was like murder. And oh God, what was that scent? Not the oranges. Something else. It was the scent of what? What? He remembered it.

'Just tell me one thing,' she insisted.

'What thing is that?'

'Tell me really what you thought of your cake. Did you actually enjoy it?'

'It was only a bloody cake.'

'Poor bloody little cake,' she said sadly. 'Here is another one.' She picked up her own cake and parted the two halves, revealing the crystallized cherry which she put on a teaspoon and offered to him.

'Fruit and quinces. Cherry and apricot,' sang in her head, and then as he waved it away, *'come, that I be no more alone.'*

'No, I missed the icon thing,' he said. 'I would have like to have seen it. As a matter of fact I was ill.'

'I can't imagine you being ill,' she said. 'You are never ill. What was the matter?'

'Oh, a virus, I think.'

'A virus?'

'Of course I get ill like everyone else from time to time. I'm not immune to illness.'

'But for this virus you would have gone to the exhibition? If you had, we would both have been there. The wife and the mistress.'

'I suppose that could have happened.'

'What would you have done?'

'Well, it was over by then.'

'Over with Rose?'

'Yes.'

'And over with me.'

He stood up. 'Thanks for the tea,' he said, 'and the cake. I must go. I'm late.'

And, after all, she did not need him or want him in her life any more. She had learned to live in her burrow. She had friends, she went to concerts and, of course, exhibitions; she travelled abroad every year. She bought the first mimosa of the season. He would only upset all of that. He would only make her miserable as he had before. She would have to let him go out into the London throng and lose him for ever.

He hesitated. 'I might see you at the Pre-Raphaelites.'

She said, 'Or Rose.'

She showed him to the door. She washed up the cups and plates. She emptied the broken up coquette au café into the bin along with the peelings of carrot and apple cores and other bits and pieces of unwanted rubbish.

SUNDAY LUNCH WITH OLIVER

~

Jo Hughes

Here's what we did on Sundays. We would leave our house at about two o'clock and walk diagonally across Ealing Common. This was just after the hurricane in 1987 and we liked to take a look at the fallen trees which, like over-delicate virgins, had fainted in the high winds. We'd pass the pub where I used to be a barmaid and where I once served Mike Oldfield of Tubular Bells fame a fat slice of savoury pie and a pint of Guinness. It was the sort of pub where they made you wear a really silly and unflattering uniform – probably to enhance your servility and invisibility in the presence of the likes of Mike Oldfield, and yes, dear reader – it worked.

But still that was all in the past and now we just walk by the pub sneering mildly.

Now we are in a deep thicket of middle class housing. The avenues are tree lined and quiet and the people are 'comfortable' except for those with redundancies and negative equity. Not many people about on these streets. It's as if Ealing has been neutron bombed and we're just waiting for the Russians to move in and take advantage of the hedge-trimmers, home computers, microwave ovens, Alessi kettles and Phillip Stark lemon squeezers.

We're just crossing the road, again diagonally, when half-way over Oliver stops walking and tugs on my arm, so I stop too.

'What?' I say and I glance around on the lookout for traffic. But it is so quiet you don't even need eyes to know when there is a car coming.

'Isn't it weird,' says Oliver. And that's a very typical Oliver type thing to say. He's always pointing out weird and strange stuff. Shooting stars or a pair of strangers on the tube who are wearing the exact same outfit, or an insect in the garden that Oliver swears is some foreign invader or hybrid.

'*So* weird,' he says, 'there's just no one around. You'd swear they were all dead or something.' The only sign of life is a smell of roast lamb and it's making me both nostalgic and hungry. It makes me think about my Mum – dead now for over fifteen years.

I tell Oliver that, and he nods thoughtfully.

We're still standing in the middle of the road. I'm waiting for Oliver to make some sort of move. And Oliver? Who knows what Oliver is waiting for?

'I'm starving,' I say in the hope this will jog Oliver's memory as to why we're here.

'Shhhh,' he says, and he waves his left palm at me like a fleshy metronome, while with his other hand he cups his chin and scratches at his three day growth of beard.

It is so quiet I can hear the sound it makes. 'Scrit, scrit, scrat,' it goes, and I think that I'd hear it even if I was up in that attic room with the open window.

'How much money do you have?' he says finally.

'Erm, six maybe seven quid.' I'm lying, as I always do with Oliver, because he never seems to appreciate the importance of keeping a bit of money for tomorrow or the day after or the day after that. I've got nearly twenty pounds in my purse, twelve quid on the mantelpiece in the rabbit jug, and two twenty pound notes between the pages of *Cooking in a Bedsit*.

He scratches some more, and I scan the road up and down to check for cars. My eye grazes the windows around us. I half expect someone to be looking down on us in our middle-of-the-road craziness.

'So,' he says 'whose turn is it to buy dinner?'

This is such a ridiculous question I almost scream with laughter, but I stifle it. In those days me or love or stupidity was always stifling the truth, though back then I called it kindness.

'Well,' I say gently, 'I think I've bought it for the last couple of weeks.' This is a big fat lie. I've bought it week after week, month after month. He last paid for dinner in February, but that occasion seems to be stuck in his mind with such clarity that he always imagines it was only two weeks ago.

'Okay,' he says 'so it must be my turn to supply dinner.'

I note that he has suddenly stopped talking about *paying* for dinner and is only offering to supply it, which knowing Oliver could mean an impromptu *dejeuner sur l'herbe* around the back of the supermarket with delicious morsels of bruised fruit and other past-its-sell-by-date fare.

More chin scratching follows, then he suddenly grabs my hand and tugs me off down the street. When we get to the main road, instead of taking the left turning towards the cafe, he turns right and ploughs on at speed until he reaches the metal stand where you can pick up free copies of *The Ealing Advertiser*. He picks up a stack of about thirty and dumps them in my arms. He then picks up a further seven or eight for himself. And off we go down the road again.

Do I ask him what is going on? Do I protest? Do I say 'Look, forget all this, I'll pay for dinner. I'd love to pay for dinner, in fact, let's have our dinner at The Grange and we can have a couple of pints as well!'

Do I say any of this? No, because part of me is a damn fool in love and the other part of me is burning with curiosity and adventure.

I'm struggling to keep up with him, my arms are aching with the load he's given me. I'm sweating in the heat and

I'm going to be a mass of black smutty smudges from the newsprint, but I'm grinning like an idiot and so thrilled to be alive and with Oliver on a day like today that I could burst.

We get back to the quiet street, and Oliver stops. 'Okie-dokie,' he says, 'here we go. You say nothing, just smile. *Comprende*?'

'*Si amigo*,' I say.

'That's Spanish!' he says, somewhat disgusted. 'I was speaking Italian.'

'Oh,' I say, feeling a little crestfallen.

'See,' he goes on, 'I ask you to say nothing and look what happens.'

'But . . .' I begin. He waves my protest away, frowning angrily, but then finishes up with one of his most delectable winks. Ah, 'the lovable rogue'. He knows how to entrap me.

I imagine his plan involves us trying to sell the free newspaper, but I can't imagine we'll make much money that way, or any at all.

Oliver trots smartly up the front steps of the first house. I follow. There's four doorbells lined up vertically to the right of the door. Oliver pushes one of his newspapers through the letterbox and trots down the steps again. We repeat this exercise several times.

The sky is blue and filled with very pure, very white and puffy clouds. A car cruises slowly down the street driven by a grey-haired man who looks too old to drive. The cooking smells are now onions and gravy. My stomach churns and creaks as if to say, 'Hey, what happened to dinner? I was expecting it! You promised!'

By the time we've delivered the free paper to the eighth house I am growing impatient.

'Olly,' I start to say, 'Olly . . .'

But we're at door number nine (number 66 actually) and Oliver is grinning and nodding.

'Here we go!' he says and he seems happy about something, though I don't see any difference between this door and the others. Oliver takes a deep breath, he's standing in what looks like his version of the official pose, arms by his side, chest puffed out, weight evenly distributed between his two desert boot clad feet. I fold one of the newspapers and offer it to him. He clucks disapproval at this and reaches for the doorbell, pushes it.

Somewhere far inside the house we hear a faint two note chime. We wait. I follow Oliver's lead and stand smartly to attention, though I'd actually like to put the newspapers down and loll on the steps with my legs stretched out.

A minute passes. He rings the bell again, then again. Far away there's a ding-dong, then another ding-dong. Oliver squats down, opens the letterbox and peers in. Next he puts his nose close to the opening and sniffs. He stands up and taps the metal knocker against the casing. 'Rat-tat-tat,' he goes. Then he gets melodic with a 'rat-tat-ta-tat-tat-ding-dong!'

No one comes to the door.

I notice that this entrance is not as well kept as the others. It's painted a dull brown and there is something tired and dusty about the place. There is no burglar alarm, no cars in the drive, only one dustbin and one bell.

Oliver is fiddling with the lock, and I think, Oh my God, he's breaking in. Oliver's a burglar and somehow I fail to see that I am a burglar too. How can I explain to anyone that I watched him and followed him into the house, as if I was merely the camerawoman, the moving eye dispassionately recording the scenes for posterity; that I was not involved, I was the detached observer.

The door swings open and we step into the chilly gloom of the hallway. Oliver pulls the door to behind me. I feel goose bumps rise along my arms and I shiver.

We stand next to each other in the hallway listening to the silence, listening to each other's breathing, listening to the music of our sin. And we grin at each other and are about to do whatever it is Oliver has planned, when we hear a sound. Or a series of sounds, rather. First we hear a thud, thud, thud, then a kind of high pitched mew. Then the thud, thud again. The thud sounds like a sort of rubber-tipped wooden stick being banged against a lino-covered floor. It sounds like that because that's what it is.

I make for the exit, but Oliver grabs my arm and gestures towards the stair. We begin to climb, at first tiptoeing, then clumping noisily. Oliver calls out, 'Hello-o.' It's his official voice. The mewing echoes the word sound, if not the precise detail. We're getting closer and my fear is falling from me now, because it seems as if the voice is calling us, willing us to it.

I suppose I had at that moment entered Oliver's madness, yet I would not have called it that. I'd have called it bravery or risk-taking or living life to the full. We should have been arrested, we should have been locked away and had our heads examined, but the weight of punishment or censorship failed to descend on our light-as-air selves.

The noises came from the top floor of the house and as we advanced toward them I felt a nervous excitement that was more like joy than fear. The mewing noises echoed and fed that feeling; the sounds increased in both pitch and frequency and lost the question mark that had at first coloured them.

The door to the room where she lay was open, but she was not immediately visible. Oliver called out, 'Hello-oh,' as he entered and I followed in my lame way.

The room was stuffed with furniture, too much furniture for one small room. There were three large wardrobes, a single bed, a double bed, two dressing tables, a standard lamp, a gate-leg table and several large packing cases. Oliver found her lying between one of the beds and a wardrobe, one of her legs trapped by a fallen box of oddments.

'I fell,' she whispered. 'I fell. You saved me. I fell. I'm old, but I can manage. Don't tell my son. Everyone falls sometimes.'

Oliver hushed her and together the two of us helped her onto the bed.

'You saved me,' she said. 'You saved my life. I fell. Don't tell. Saved me . . .'

Not for one moment did she wonder at our being there; we were there to save her. We were her saviours. Her guardian angels. Oliver was a darling boy.

We checked her for injuries. Asked her if she felt sick or dizzy. Did she have any pain? Then we gave her instructions – lift this leg, wiggle your toes. She obliged us, smiling all the while. She was fine, she said and, indeed, she did seem so.

We helped her downstairs.

'How long had you been trapped there?' I asked. I expected an answer of hours or days.

'Oh, only a few minutes, but then you came. I knew you would. He sent you, didn't he?'

I don't know who she meant by 'he' – the son or God?

Neither Oliver nor I answered the question, and we tried to change the subject. I mentioned a doctor. Oliver mentioned lunch.

'Now then,' he said, and he was stern and efficient. 'Have you eaten? I wouldn't be surprised to find that your fall was due to hunger. Have you had lunch?'

She meekly shook her head.

'Ah ha,' he said, triumphant. 'Then Lizzie and I will have to cook you some. Won't we, Lizzie?'

Lunch was strange that day; boiled potatoes, ham from a three-sided tin with oval edges, a fried egg, tinned peas, followed by tea and ancient biscuits.

'Next week,' she promised, 'we'll have a proper roast. Pork, crackling, stuffing, roast potatoes, gravy, mashed potatoes, apple sauce, cabbage, peas, carrots and tapioca pudding to finish.'

Oliver grinned and she called him her own darling boy again. They seemed to have bonded in dreams; on some abstract astral plane where old ladies were always saved, and darling boys got fed. Promises were made about next week, about trips to the supermarket and tea on Wednesday. I imagined it all; our kindness, us moving in, caring for her – though caring in my mind consisted only of a lot of hand-holding and brow-mopping. Good Lord, she'd probably end up leaving us the house in her will. This was forever, I thought. Maybe we were meant to save her, maybe fate or God or whatever isn't just rolling dice, but planning ahead. Maybe.

By the following Sunday Oliver was dead.

He had been out with his friends in Islington. Drunk, yes, but not that drunk. They were crossing the road, three ran across and two stayed on the pavement waiting, and Oliver, not quite sure which group he belonged to, hesitated fatally, then darted into the path of a lorry.

No one was there to save him. The voice of fate was muffled by two pints of Stella, three bottles of Grolsch and a single whisky chaser. She had watched over him for nearly twenty-six years. The darling boy had eaten up all his luck and there were no more Sunday dinners, no more lies and second chances.

HOME COOKING

~

Lynne Rees

No one admits to what it's really like. They talk about the freedom, the quiet, the lack of washing and ironing, about not lying in bed gone midnight waiting to hear a key in the door. They all use phrases like 'At last!' and 'What a relief!' But you can tell they don't believe themselves. The laughs stop in their throat, and their eyes, their eyes give them away. They are aching with the absence, the vacuum in the house, like something's been irretrievably lost, or stolen.

I am aching. And she's only been gone five days.

It's not as if the house is empty either – Jez is still racketing around his bedroom, his speakers belching out sounds I find hard to identify as music.

'Red Hot Chilli Peppers,' he says.

'That figures.'

I didn't go to the airport. I couldn't, I said. I was working. But I could have asked for a few hours off. She was sitting in front of the gas fire in the living room and stretched up on her knees to hug me around the waist before I left. There are a thousand things I could have said – I'll miss you, I love you, You are everything to me. But the words were jammed in my throat. I said, 'Keep safe. Ring me when you get there.'

I can't eat – my stomach tightens and resists when I try to force food down. It was Catherine I cooked for. Jez has looked after himself for months now – tossing pizzas and veggie burgers into the microwave. At least I still manage to persuade him to eat some fruit. And David eats his three-course subsidised lunches in the staff canteen and only ever wants a snack in the evening. No, it was Catherine who relied on me to sit at the table with her every weekday evening at seven. And she never complained, never poked anything around her plate, always ate every single scrap, put her knife and fork down with, 'Thanks, Mam.' It felt like our time.

A couple of years ago, just after her eighteenth birthday, she fell ill. She spent weeks in bed sleeping for most of the day and night. The only things she would eat and drink were grated cheese and tomato sandwiches and hot chocolate. The doctor eventually diagnosed glandular fever but only after mis-prescribing penicillin, so she woke up one morning covered in red weals. I took those sandwiches up the stairs every day twice a day for three weeks. When she eventually agreed to eat something else, I tried mixing a raw egg into buttery mashed potato just to get some goodness into her, but she said she could taste it and she was too ill for me to argue with her. That was so much like her – sensitive, particular, strong-willed, or just plain stubborn.

She called me the first night. She was staying in a hotel until the flat was ready at the end of the week. She had to go shopping with the girl she'd be sharing with. I smiled to myself – now that I'd like to see. Not the Pantene shampoo, fat free yoghurts, and Tesco's 40 denier opaque black tights shopping she did for herself here, but real-life shopping – all purpose cleaner, toilet rolls, milk, bread, spread. All the things she'd found ready to hand in cupboards, or in the fridge, up until now. I imagined what their food cupboard would look like – a shelf of stark melamine supporting a tin of Chicken Tonight Sauce and a jar of mixed herbs that probably wouldn't be opened before the sell-by date, but seemed like the sort of thing they should buy when they saw it on the supermarket shelf. Somehow homely and familiar. I thought to myself, she'll be calling me every other day, wanting to know how to cook this and that, what number to roast a chicken on, and how long for. She'll still need me, my voice, my experience of feeding a husband, and then two kids, three times a day for a total of twenty-two years. She'll be calling, I thought.

But once she's in her flat, after I call her the first day her new phone's connected to check to see if she's all right, and she laughs at me for worrying and says she'll speak to me soon. I don't hear from her for nearly three weeks. And then Sunday there's her voice, perky as anything.

'Hi, Mam.'

'What do you mean "Hi!",' I say abruptly, 'do you realise it's three weeks since we last spoke, and then it was I who called you?'

There's a fat silence on the line, only seconds, but I can feel its weight. It's not what I wanted to say. Not what I planned to say, but out it came when I heard her – so happy, so bright, breaking into the monochrome of my Sunday morning.

'I've been busy at work,' she says. 'You know that. And doing up the flat.'

She rushes on, barrelling through the silence.

'We met two guys working here for the summer and we agreed we'd cook them dinner every night for a week, in exchange for them putting up some shelves and painting the bathroom.'

My daughter cooking meals for men! I imagine a variation of things on toast.

'What on earth did you give them?' My voice is still brittle.

'Just ordinary stuff. Sausage and mash, jacket potatoes, spaghetti bolognese. But one night we forgot to go shopping so they had to put up with tomato soup and cheese on toast.'

'And you?' I force myself to say. 'Are you eating properly?'

'Of course I am. But I'm out for lunch today. And we've had auditors in the Dealing Room and they took me out for dinner on Friday. The restaurants are brilliant over here, Mam. Have you ever tried guinea-fowl?'

My daughter is living a life I have never even imagined. What does guinea-fowl taste like? What does it even look like?

Another two weeks go by and she calls to tell me she's just given her first dinner party.

'All from a book. But it turned out great.'

She takes me through her menu. *Pommes Dauphinoise* – sliced potatoes cooked in layers with onion, cheese and cream. And a leg of lamb basted with Marsala. I don't even know what Marsala is.

'It's a sweet wine. A bit like port. I only picked it because it looked like the easiest recipe in the book. And the potatoes, they cook right down. I could have done with some more really.'

I couldn't have told her that. I couldn't have warned her that would happen even if she had called for my advice. I have never done anything more extravagant to a potato than roasted it.

She and her flatmate invest in weekly editions of Robert Carrier's *Creative Cookery*. She tells me about Chicken Satay with Sweet Peanut Sauce and Cucumber Salad. She laughs at the amount of sieving Carrier demands and says she's already thought of an easier way to do it next time. But she'll make the strawberry shortcake again, everybody loved it; fragile discs of biscuit layered with fresh strawberries and vanilla-flavoured cream.

I notice that I'm eating more normally now, orange juice and coffee at breakfast, a sandwich for lunch. I ask David if he can just have a snack at work and I make an effort to do a proper dinner for us when he gets home. Jez carries on with his instant food regime.

Tonight I get my *Reader's Digest Cookery Year Book* out. The pages still smell new and the ribbon marker is still in the section for January, the same place as when it arrived three years ago. I look up *Pommes Dauphinoise*. Waxy potatoes, gruyere cheese, it says, finely chopped onions, single cream, freshly ground black pepper.

'Do you like gruyere cheese?' I ask David who's just settling down for the nine o'clock news with a can of lager.

'Never heard of it. What's it taste like?'

'I don't know. Catherine told me about it.'

'Ah well, she's an international banker now.'

He smiles at me for a couple of seconds longer than he needs to. I dream of her stalking across Europe, a caravan of exotic food and wines – lobsters, truffles, mangoes, a snuffling group of pungent French cheeses – jostling behind her, like the clatter of tins people tie to the rear bumpers of wedding cars.

On Saturday I ask the woman at the cheese counter in Tesco's if I can have a taste of the gruyere. I want to tell David what it's like. But it's unfamiliar on my tongue, like nothing I have ever had in my life.

SHARON

~

Chloe Heuch

My sister was the one who cried. I was sweet and silent as
a wish, my mum said. When she went for her first scan the
hospital didn't recognise two heartbeats, but Mum said she
knew there were two all along. People would marvel over
Sharon and me, lying side by side: at our double set of perfect
hands, our two pairs of wide dark eyes. No one had seen
identical twins before, Mum said.

Sharon has the same tea-coloured hair as me. She has the
same eyes – sometimes green, sometimes hazel. When she
smiles she shows the same gap between her teeth. We did
everything together: started our periods, took the same
subjects at school, achieved the same grades. We even lost
our virginity at the same time. Together forever.

No. I'm sorry. That isn't the story at all, though I wish it was.
All of those things, they happened to me. Just me. Amanda
Thackery, spoilt only child of Gwen and David Thackery.
Amanda Thackery, quiet and lonely, the one and only. There
has only been me. For twenty years. No other. No reflection.
No mirror girl for me to look into and find the truth. No
Sharon. Mum's shape froths up behind the frosted glass of
No. 29. I can tell she has her hair down for the special
occasion. She opens the front door.

'Happy Birthday, darling!' There is no time to take her in
before she has me clamped to her, her dark hair mingling
with mine, her soft cheek against my face. 'Twenty-one

today!' She holds me slightly away from her. 'Look at you, grown up girl.'

'Mum!' I smile.

Dad stands in the shadows of the hall. He gives me a bear hug and pecks my cheek. 'Happy Birthday, Amanda.'

'Thanks, Dad.'

She whispers conspiratorially in my ear, 'We were worried about the trains. I said to your father, he should've gone to get you.'

'They were fine, Mum. I got here okay.'

'Yes, well.' She ushers me in front of her into the lounge.

The dining table is laid all ready for my birthday feast. At the heart of the table is an enormous bowl of sharon fruit. No other choice in the bowl. These strange fruit have always shared my birthdays, my poor mother's way of marking the anniversary. 'Sharon's fruit,' I used to call them. I didn't know then I even had a sister. There was the mystery, right in front of my eyes all along.

They watch me open the presents. It has always been this way. Me and them.

'It's beautiful, Mum, Dad. Thanks.' I hold up the silver locket and see it glinting.

'Open it.'

Inside there is a tiny picture of Mum, Dad and me on holiday in Cornwall.

'Aah, that's lovely,' I say.

Would Mum have kept it from me forever, I wonder, the knowledge I had a twin and the awful tragedy of how I lost her? I found out by accident. I asked for my birth certificate; she keeps hold of it for me, so I won't lose it. She was looking through her box of papers, sat on their bed, and Dad was out, I can't remember where; I know the house was still and quiet except for her fingering through all those important things in that shoe box. The phone rang. She ran downstairs to get it. I was bored of waiting so I picked up the cardboard box and idled through the documents, the letters and the photographs.

I was only really interested in the pictures. There were silly ones of me upside down, face all purple. Dad looking huffy on the golf course. Granny and Grandad Hughes, who aren't alive any more.

In a white envelope were some baby pictures. In each there were two babies, one the reflection of the other. I knew I was one of them. I had seen myself before in old photos and my baby blanket, the one I still have with the balloon bears on it, was wrapped around me. Us. Which one was me? The faces were identical.

Mum was at the door, red and silent. She didn't say anything. She snatched the photos off me and drove off in the car. It was only when Dad returned home that I found out the terrible truth.

It was cot death. Took my sister from me. Cot death crept up in the night and with his blind hands suffocated her, stole her away from us.

'Right, dinner then. It won't cook itself.' Mum jumps up and clears away the wrapping paper.

'Your mother's cooking roast pork, Amanda, just for you.'

'Lovely.'

'Let me top you up first.' My dad is delaying Mum's exit. He slops golden liquid into all our glasses. Then Mum is off into the kitchen to bat this into that, making it nice. Just for me. 'How's uni, Amanda?' Dad leans back into a cushion.

'Finals next month,' I groan.

'I hope you're revising!'

'Mmm.' I grin at him. There is a pause as he tips back his sherry glass.

My eyes strain to the small orange rounds in the bowl on the table, each one separate, identical. I want to pick one up, feel it. I want to understand its difference. The rule has always been never to touch, never to eat. It never struck me how bizarre it was, to keep these untouchable fruit as an ornament, to smack small hands that strayed into the bowl. I thought Mum kept them for the colour, if I thought of it at all. It was just how it was.

'Amanda! Can you give me a hand?' Mum's voice calls from the kitchen. Dad beams at me teasingly. Normally I would have complained about having to help on my birthday, but it is different today. Everything has changed.

The kitchen is all vegetable steam.

'Just pour those in there, will you?' I grab the potatoes off the cooker.

She busies herself with the cauliflower, allowing butter to slide onto the florets, greasing them yellow. 'Right, can you just put the lids on the tureens, then pop them on the table, love, please?'

I trundle through with the dishes and arrange them around the sharon fruit. Dad must have gone to the toilet. The room is empty. I so want to take one of the fruits, but it would feel like a betrayal. I return to the kitchen.

Mum continues beating the gravy, her head down. I notice how dry and heavy she looks. It strikes me that I have never seen her cry. She sloops the gravy into the boat.

I clear my throat. 'They don't know what causes it, do they? Cot death. Apparently it can be the way babies lie when they're asleep, or if the mother smokes, but they don't really know. Mum? They don't really know, do they? What causes it.' She chooses this moment to open the oven door and I lose her in a cloud of steam and sizzle as she pulls out the enormous roast.

'Sorry, love, what did you say?'

It's no use. She will not talk to me. 'Nothing.'

'I knew I'd forgotten something. Can you put the apple sauce into the jug, love.'

I sit down at the breakfast bar and dole out lumps of green into the blue and white jug. I thought last night it could have so easily been me that died. It could have been Sharon celebrating her birthday, helping her mum, who is my mum. My mum with her floral shirt and cords – I used to get so embarrassed by those cords. She used to drop me off at school in them, a real hippy, with her leather jacket and her giant plait of hair down her back. Now I'm glad she's like that. When I was small, if I was upset she would rock me on her lap. I would cuddle her plait of hair and all my tears would drizzle down her neck. She never complained. That bit of skin, where her neck meets her shoulder bone, is so soft.

If it was me that died I would want people to talk about me.

'I'm serving up now. You coming?'

'Yes, I'm starving.'

The sharon fruit stay central, even though there's hardly an inch to spare for all the food on the table. They always stay on the table for the whole birthday day, and then they disappear. We eat across the bowl. Dad is talking about Greece, when Mum and he went and their bags got lost. I think he's trying to keep everyone cheerful.

I wonder about Dad: how could he have kept quiet about Sharon? He's such a blabber mouth. He forgets what he's supposed to say and what he's not. What was it like for him? I found something about cot death on the internet at work. This woman had photographs of her dead baby boy and poems about him. She said she felt like her heart had been ripped out. She said when you lose a child you lose the future. That woman, she has sympathy, cards and a grave-stone to lay flowers, she has a family there, grieving with her. She doesn't have to pretend everything is okay. I look and see how brittle my mother is. I notice the way her eyes dart about, so no one can catch her off guard.

Mum assumes I don't remember Sharon. It is impossible to remember her physically, not even from the photographs. Four months old. I do remember, though, in a different way; it is difficult to explain. An absence. Part of my mind. We were made from the same cell, the same fruit of my mother's womb.

'Were me and Sharon the same?' I ask over my pork roast.

There is a pause. Dad looks at Mum, unsure now the rules have changed.

'Like peas from the same pod, love,' he says with a wistful smile.

'I know we looked the same, but were we the same people?'

'What do you mean, Mand?'

Mum watches me.

'Were we the same?' I look at the fruit in the bowl. Identical. 'Did we – I mean , the personalities. I know we were only babies. What was she like?'

'Oh Amanda,' Mum breathes out. Words in a breath.

'Sharon was a fighter, love. She came out kicking.' My Dad's eyes focus beyond the room. 'She was the first out, screaming her head off. You followed, quiet as a lamb.' He returns to me, wavers and glances at Mum. 'She was the first to do everything and up all night, kept your mother busy, she did.' He chuckles to himself. 'You were your Mum's blessing. You kept her sane.'

'We weren't the same, then?'

'Sharon had her ways. You had yours. That was clear from the start.' He smiles. I notice how soft and wet his eyes are.

'Did we get on?'

There is a pause. Dad forks a potato and chews it thoughtfully. I start to cut a thick of piece of meat, for Mum's sake rather than out of any sense of hunger.

'You used to play with each other's fingers when you lay next to each other, smiling at each other and giggling together. You watched each other all the time. We used to wake in the morning and find you both looking into each other's eyes. You loved each other.' He seems glad to talk. I watch the fleeting expressions wash over his face.

'Yes,' I say.

'You cried for months after she'd gone. You wouldn't eat. It was very difficult.' He looks up sharply at the scrape of Mum's chair.

She gets up from the table and makes for the door. She is trying to stop those heavy tears from coming. I'm not going to let her get away. I reach her and hug her stone body. I hold on. I feel something break. That hard core inside. It is her tears drizzling down my neck, me, her grown-up daughter. The one that lived, holding her like a baby, as she cries and cries and cries.

A sharon fruit is shaped like a beef tomato, but it is hard and smooth. It smells of delicate citrus. The skin is quite tight like an apple, but an orange colour. Mum gave me one to take home this evening. I cut a sliver on the blue ceramic, taste the peel, then taste the flesh. It has a hint of melon, and it reminds me of carrot if carrots were soft; such a mixture of different traits and qualities, too many to be a hybrid. It is an original fruit. I cut another piece. And another. Inside, there seems to be no pips, only occasional softer threads of taste, but no core, no hard centre. I eat it all. I like it.

MA MAISON

~

Julia Gregson

On June 16, their eighth wedding anniversary, Tim and
Jody Rossiter drove their battered Ford towards their
favourite restaurant, *Ma Maison*, in the Blue Mountains. It
was quite a hike from Sydney – two hours and ten minutes
door to door – Tim had taken to timing such things. Tim and
Jody, who'd emigrated from England five years before, still
found it hard to accept the distances one had to travel here
to find places of the heart.

The restaurant sat on top of a hill that was nearly a mountain, near a spa town called Wentworth Falls. You drove
down an unmarked road and then saw the biggest, bluest,
most drunkenly virtiginous view you ever saw in your life,
and beside it a simple, colonial-style house with a veranda
and a sign:

'*Ma Maison, prop: Henri Guitton.*'

In the spring and summer you could sit on the veranda
and admire the blue skeins of mist on the pine-scented hills
and imagine yourself in a Japanese print. In winter, when
Henri lit a big fire and the winds roared, *Ma Maison*, with its
marvellous food, its tinkling glasses, its bursts of music and
talk, was a kernel of sanity and happiness in a difficult world.
Henri himself was an emigre from Provence, a large, pale,
serious man with a smile of great innocence and sweetness.
There were no false mine hosty flourishes in him. No need
for teeth and twinkles to make up for what the food lacked.
He shook your hand with the proper blend of festivity and

authority, for his menu was simple and perfect. He was fanatical about the ingredients he chose. The herby, salty lamb he served had been fed on salt bushes near Broken Hill. Chickens and eggs came from a woman in Leura, olive oil from the Hunter Valley, coriander and fresh fennel from his own garden, and from his kitchens emerged amazing puddings: tarte au citron, fresh sorbets, chocolate mousses and creme caramels of such dreamlike lightness that even sophisticated customers would audibly groan.

Tim and Jody, lit up with anticipation, walked across the car park towards the inn. A young girl in a long starched apron greeted them. She took them to a table in the corner of the room, near a fire. The room, candle-lit, garlic-scented, glowed and hummed with life. On each table was a small blue glass jug with an arrangement of yellow lilies.

'The especial today,' said the girl, who was pretty but pale, 'is John Dory, seared wiz a couli of peppers and garlic. Rack of lamb wiz mange toute and Henri's new potatoes, and for dessert creme caramel, chocolate mousse, tarte aux peches.'

Jody saw Tim literally shiver with delight and in that gesture saw the young husband who had first brought her here. Twenty-two years old, in a tweed jacket brought for school, broke, but determined to bless their arrival in Australia with what was, in those days, an insanely expensive meal.

Now Tim frowned at the wine list in his half-moon specs. '*You'll* want champagne,' he said.

'Do you?'

'I suppose so.' The grudging voice was a husbandly joke.

She smiled, then made him frown by saying, 'We could go halves.' This year, for the first time ever, her salary as a teacher outstripped his, but the rules for special evenings out were still not clear.

'The Chardonnay,' said Tim to the waitress. When she'd

gone, he confided, in the broad Australian accent he had perfected, 'All the draaama of Shakespeare with the homely qualities of nat naaasties.'

His being silly almost made up for the disappointment of the champagne, which she had looked forward to. The expensive bubbles, the celebratory glow. Childish, she told herself, when money was tight.

When the wine came, he drank half a glass fast. 'I needed that,' he said.

They looked away from each other. Tim's architectural practise, begun with such high hopes eight years ago, was losing money. Recently he'd been offered a job in New Zealand. When he'd told her, so casually it hurt, she'd had an image of herself being lifted lifeless and smiling across another continent, like a doll or a ballerina.

'So how's our little rug rat?' he said. Talking about Cassie was good. She'd started school that term and was achingly proud of her new navy skirt, of the new leather satchel which swamped her. She'd run from their arms towards the school bus on her spindly white legs, shouting, 'Boy Mum, Boy Ded,' as if she'd lived here all her life.

'She's made new friends,' said Jody, 'and she wants to bring them home for tea. She's given me an enormous list of what they'll need – Iced vovos, Violet crumbles, Jam Jerimiahs. All the Aussie biscuits.'

Tim looked stricken. 'My child will never know the splendours of a Chocolate Bath Oliver, of a Rich Tea.'

'Rubbish,' she said. 'We'll have a holiday and she can chomp her way around the British Isles.'

'Great idea. A two thousand dollar packet of biscuits.'

Another dawning realisation – they could no longer afford to go home.

'Henri? Where's Henri?' she said suddenly. The girl in the apron was nowhere to be seen.

'He's a busy man. Fifteen tables here between twenty-five and fifty dollars a head. That's a useful chunk of change.' This was a new habit of Tim's – translating every experience into profit and loss.

'I'm so hungry,' she said.

'And it's late.' Tim checked his watch. 'By the time we get down that mountain, it will be past midnight.'

'I'll look for him.' She left the table, feeling slightly elevated and unreal after two glasses of wine. Her feet glided like canisters across the polished floor and the rugs, towards the dark swing doors and then into the mouth of the kitchen, where she stood, suddenly shy, calling, 'Henri?'

It felt like forbidden territory and then, through clouds of steam, she saw Henri sitting in the middle of a shambles of slung plates and snarled tablecloths. His whole body sagged. There was a bottle of brandy in front of him. She thought he was laughing, then she saw he was weeping, terrible tears right down from his bootstraps.

'Henri, my love. Whatever's the matter?'

He lifted his head and shook it slowly. 'Please –' he tried to wave her away with a smile – 'Just bugger off.'

'Henri.' She put her arms around him.

'Mrs Rossiter.' He suddenly collapsed against her and sobbed in hollow booms into her bosom. 'My mother is dead. She died this morning.'

She held him close and listened to the grinding of his teeth, his heart, his whole inner mechanism.

'You should have closed.'

'I had to stay open. What else have I got?' His huge brown eyes were muddied with grief, his eyebrows almost vertical. 'But I can't! I can't do it!'

Over his shoulder a sauce bubbled over, slid down the side of a saucepan.

'Where are your helpers, Henri?'

'I told her to piss off and stop looking at me like a dead fish.'

'Henri, you didn't!' She was horrified. 'Why were you so rude?'

'I'm always like that.' His tears ran faster. 'I'm horrible, and now I lose my mother, my staff and my customers.'

With a wild look at her, he passed out with a thump over the table. A glass of Armanac dripped onto the floor and over her shoes.

'Henri!' She put her face close to his ear and spoke distinctly. 'Tell me what to do.'

'Tray up veggie for table two.' His voice seemed to come from a great distance. 'Bill for table five, extra coffee. Smile. Thank you very much, good night.' With his head down on his hands and his mouth all open and squidgy, he slept again, a large, sad, fat baby worn out with tears.

Jody stood in the mouth of the restaurant and made her announcement. 'Excuse me everyone, but M. Guitton is unwell. If I can help you with your orders, please let me know.' There were six tables of diners left. In the smokey glow of the room their faces came back to her, pale and distorted. Tim looked owlish in his astonishment. She made her way towards him, pad in hand.

'What the hell's going on?'

'Henri's passed out in the kitchen. His mother died yesterday.'

'Here?'

'No, in France.'

'Oh my God.' Tim, whose 83-year-old mother lived in sheltered accommodation in Worthing, understood. 'What a nightmare.' He shook his head and drained his glass. 'Poor bloody man.'

'If I was you, mate, I'd liquidate the losses,' said the man at the next table to his friend. He'd barely looked up during her announcement. 'Miss,' he said. 'Bill, please.'

She found it on a spike near the till, and collected a further sixty-five dollars from table five plus five dollars for herself. 'Good night, good night,' she cried as she put on their coats and eased them into the swirling mists. 'God bless, come back soon.'

When the last customer was gone, and there was a satisfying wad of notes in the till, Tim came up behind her and put his arms around her waist. He kissed her behind the ear. 'Nice waitress, great ass,' he murmured.

He was quite drunk and considerably more cheerful.

Back in the kitchen, Henri was asleep on a pile of dirty tablecloths. Between them, they dragged him upstairs, his legs swinging on the floor. On the landing they tried various doors into dusty rooms. The third room on the right had an iron bed with crates of soda and soft drinks underneath. It was tiny and smelled of damp.

'Poor Henri.' She was shocked. They propped him against the wall. She untied his apron and eased it over his head.

Tim helped him into blue and white pyjamas. They tipped him into bed. She put on his bedside lamp. There were burn marks from old cigarettes on the table. It was starting to rain outside.

'Shall I go down and get him a drink?' said Tim.

'That would be kind.'

When Tim had gone, Henri woke up remembering and cried, 'Maman, Maman, oh strewth.' He shook his head.

'I met her once when she came to see you,' said Jody. 'She had the most lovely brown eyes.'

'So beautiful,' Henri said. 'I tried to get her to stay here but she said she had no clothes.'

'No clothes?'

'"For that dress," she would say, "I could buy a leg of lamb, for that hat three dozen eggs."' His mouth capsized. He trembled with sorrow.

'Tim's gone to get you a drink,' she said. 'Would you like that?'

'She used to make me hot chocolate, like the one they make in *Deux Magots* with real lumps of chocolate in the milk. She gave me this.'

He took a little battered leather book from his bedside table.

'Marmite,' he read in a broken voice. He muttered words in French then said, 'Take three fresh oxtails and marinate in dry red wine. Everything I know comes from her, and while she dies, I am here, "Enjoy your meal, sir, have a nice evening." He waggled his head grotesquely and wept.

Tim came in with the rest of the bottle of Armanac, a pot of tea and some inexpertly hacked sandwiches. He was swaying, concentrating fiercely.

'Voila,' he said, 'plat du jour.'

'Perhaps Henri would prefer coffee.' She was trying to remember if French people drank tea.

Tim's face fell.

'We're quite new ourselves,' said Jody, as she poured the tea and tucked a section of Henri's duvet around her. 'When we first came to your restaurant four years ago, we'd only just arrived in Australia. It seems such a big adventure at first, the glossy brochures, the surf, the blue skies, then suddenly you're here and what's changed? Except you're washing up 12,000 miles away from home and your family's gone and everything's different and the dog's in kennels.' Tim watched Jody warily from the end of the bed. It worried him, her new habit of confiding in near strangers.

'And we were walking one day,' Jody went on, 'across the valley below here. It was freezing, nobody ever tells you it gets cold in Australia, and we found your place. You were a lot thinner then.' Henry almost smiled. 'You put us near the fire, we ate steaks, pommes frites, a salad. We couldn't believe how good it was. You put three kinds of pudding on the table, a lemon tarte, a creme caramel and that meringuey-vanilla-y thing.'

'Neige au creme.'

'You put them all out on the table, just as if we were in your house, and said, "Help yourself." That was not a small thing. I don't know how people run restaurants.' She lost her drift. 'I have visitors for two days and I get so irritable I can't wait for them to leave.'

'Madame.' Henri gripped her hand. 'I am going to tell you something now. You cannot run a good restaurant without love – it's too hard. You are on your feet for hours on end, you are hot, you're exhausted most of the time, but you are also, I don't know how to say this, you are vibing. All those people have come to you for a special reason. They are falling in love, they are dying, they are about to be sacked, or have the best fuck of their lives, or make a lot of money, and it all comes through you.'

He closed his eyes and shook his head like a big tree absorbing wind. 'Fair dinkum, that's why you can stay up so late and not fall down.'

'Your Mother –' Jody brushed crumbs from the pillow – 'must have loved you.'

'She did.' The chef's voice was a squeak. Two lines of tears raced down his cheeks but he was smiling.

Tim watched his wife in awe: an artist, retreating, advancing, applying deft strokes of light and shade.

'Do you have a wife, a girlfriend?' she asked.

'No time,' Henri said, flirting a little from blue and white pyjamas. 'My very hot mistress has been the stove.'

Jody tutted. 'You must make more time for yourself.'

'There is a girl who helps me in the kitchen. A very lovely girl, very talented, but I am so hard on the people I work with. Tonight, I made her cry.'

'Oh Henri, that was naughty. Will you have the chance to say sorry?'

Henri's shrug was immense.

Tim lay at the other end of the bed drunk enough to feel the bed rocking slightly, like a boat sailing out into the dark and glorious night. He blazed with love for his wife, her blonde hair swinging over the collapsed chef, her courage.

He thought of the second time he'd driven her up the mountain to Henri's. She was pregnant with Cassie and slightly car sick. Her schoolgirl's skin, still pale and unlined by the Aussie sun, her blue dress. The protective giddying terror he'd felt at leading her into all this. Half way back, down the mountains again, he'd stopped the car at a look out point and held her like a bomb.

'That's my father . . . my sister . . . my house . . . my father's dog.'

At the other end of the bed Henri had found a large battered photograph album, and was going through it with Jody.

They stayed with Henri until the moon dimmed between the curtains, and he closed his eyes and fell asleep.

Jody drove Tim home down the mountains. He gazed out of the car window, at the mad wonder of it all, at the moon hurtling between the trees. He felt his infinitely precious wife beside him at the wheel, thought of Henri getting back some of the love paid for in exile and olive oil, in the flesh of lambs, in fresh flowers.

'I don't want to go to New Zealand, do you?' he said out loud.

'Not much.' She smiled.

Below them, Sydney was laid out like a vast electrical circuit, small dots of light in the dark. Jody drove towards the heart of it, while he thought of his own mother. He would phone her tomorrow. He tried to unscramble the time differences – was it subtract ten or add eleven? He could never quite remember.

PINK CAKE

~

Melanie Newman

Rosie's Dad was the nicest in the world. She loved him more
than anyone else, more than *anything* else. He was the coolest,
the most handsome, the best at games of all the Dads and he
smelled the best. She loved his eyes that crinkled at the corner
when he smiled and his white teeth that gleamed in the
darkness of his beard and his smell, that Dad smell, like no
other. Rosie loved that smell so much she stole his polo-neck
jumpers from the dirty laundry basket and carried them
around with her until the smell wore or off or her mother
took them away. She needed the sweaters to remind her
because he worked a lot, sometimes until past her bedtime;
sometimes three or even four days would go by without her
seeing him, he left so early and arrived back home so late.
She always tried to stay awake to hear him come in but
couldn't ever seem to manage it, though she never remembered falling asleep.

Sometimes, now, she awoke to the sound of raised voices,
her mother screaming. She could hear the high pitched
yammering, the sound rising and falling, without being able
to distinguish words. Then Dad's voice: a low hum, replying.
It was horrible and it was happening more often now, or
maybe she just woke more often. She burrowed to the bottom
of the bed and pulled the pillow over her head when she
heard them. It was too hot down there and it made her ears
red but it was better than listening.

The next mornings were always horrible, too. Her mother,

red-eyed, crashing around the kitchen, Dad's place at the table unlaid. Usually he left extra early on those mornings; she heard the door clunk shut behind him, leaving her alone with her mother. She ate her breakfast quickly then, her eyes fixed on her cornflakes, not looking at her mother, whose shoulders shook as she washed the dishes, and who cried noiseless tears that dripped from her nose like snot. Afterwards, when she dressed Rosie for school, she buttoned her up all wrong and (once) put her knickers on inside out. Rosie was quite able to dress herself and would have preferred to, but her mother insisted. Then she brushed Rosie's long red hair, sometimes with hard angry strokes that made her wince and sometimes softly with trembling hands, hands that seemed to be crying into her hair. The relief when she heard the bus coming, could run out of the door, bag unfastened and hair already falling out of its plaits, and leave her mother behind!

Those were the times she hated most because there was a good chance that Dad would not come home at all in the evening and the morning's atmosphere would linger after school. Even when things were normal her mother was not always nice to be around so she spent a lot of time in her room, or, in summer, in the garden. She read about girls who had imaginary friends and tried to dream up her own, but it didn't work; she knew that there was no one there and only mad people talk to empty spaces. Besides, she had the best friend anyone could want – Dad.

It was Mother's Day. When Rosie came downstairs Dad was up already.

'Good moaning Dad,' she said happily. They always said good moaning to each other; it was *their* joke. Then her mother walked in, still in her dressing gown, a milk bottle clamped under each armpit and two in each hand. Her eyes were puffy and red.

'These had better not have gone off. Out there since yesterday morning. Why is it always left to me to bring them in?' she muttered, half to herself, crashing the bottles down on the sink.

'Bird's messed on this one – Rosie, wipe them off for me, will you, and put them in the fridge. Got to get the breakfast going. It's getting late.'

Rosie picked up the bottle and gingerly touched the white streak down its side. It was hard and dry; it wouldn't even come off when she scraped it with her fingernail. So she ran it under the tap and scrubbed at it with the scourer. The water was deliciously hot on her fingers; it made her shiver and the hairs stood up on her arm.

Suddenly her mother turned from the stove and screamed at her.

'Don't use that, it's unhygienic!'

Rosie jumped and the bottle fell from her fingers into the sink and broke at the neck, the milk pulsing from it like blood from a wound.

'You stupid, you *stupid*!' Her mother flew across the room, trembling with anger.

Dad stepped in front of her and caught her hand as she lifted it. 'It was an accident,' he said. 'Anyone can drop a bottle.'

Her mother's face flushed bright red and her mouth opened but no words came out. She opened and closed it again, gasping and shuddering. Her arm drooped limply in Dad's grasp. Then the tears began to fall. It wasn't right that she should cry so much.

'I'm sorry, Rosie,' she said. 'I'm terribly, terribly sorry.'

Rosie did not look at her. She could still see the raised

hand and the picture was burning inside her. She tried to push it out of her mind but it wasn't ready to go yet. There was another memory that was an almost a year old and it still sprang into her head and made her miserable. But that was worse; that was when all this had started.

At school, earlier in the week, Rosie had refused to make a card for Mother's Day.

'But your mum loves you very much and does a lot for you and this is a way to say thank you and make her feel special,' said plump Miss Harris.

'She doesn't love me, she wishes I'd never been born,' replied Rosie and all Miss Harris's protestations could not convince her otherwise. She remembered a conversation overheard long ago when she was five. Her mother was crying again, crying at Dad, blaming him.

'If only I had known before I had Rosie. If only she hadn't been born.' Her voice was thick and choked.

'You don't mean that,' said Dad, in his deep gentle voice.

'I do, I do. If it wasn't for her I could start again, but now, now . . .'

Rosie's stomach had hurt then as it always did just before she was sick. But she was not sick and neither did she cry, though she almost did. Instead she went into the bathroom, took the nail scissors from the closet and determinedly cut up the velveteen rabbit that her mother had given her on her last birthday; the grey rabbit with the long floppy ears that had slept in her bed every night since that birthday. When she saw her beloved Rabbit in pieces on the bed, white stuffing spewing from his decapitated, earless head, her resolve nearly weakened. She almost ran to her mother to tell her what she had done, to cry against her thin chest and be sorry. But her mother's crime was too great.

'I will never forgive her,' she said to herself, aloud to give herself courage.

Now she almost hated the woman who had said she did not want her but whose shaky hands in her hair spoke of a deeper feeling that she could detect but not recognise. On Father's Day she made the most elaborate card in the class. Dad was so pleased with it that he picked her up in his arms just as he used to when she was small and squeezed her hard. Over his head she saw her mother looking at the card and her face was tight and set as though she were clenching her teeth. The next day Dad brought her a present although it wasn't her birthday and she wasn't ill. It was huge. Under the smart foil wrapping paper was a doll in a box. Only not a normal doll. This one had a white porcelain face and stiff white hands held rigidly in front of it as though it were measuring something. It wore a red velvet hat and dress trimmed with white lace. It was nearly as big as Rosie and its enormous, unblinking, blue eyes stared at her unnervingly. She wasn't at all sure what to do with it and held its cold china hand uncertainly while Dad watched, smiling, and fetched the camera for a photo. Her mother was angry afterwards; it would have to go back to the shop she said, they couldn't afford it. So Rosie hid the doll at the bottom of her toy chest; smothered it under six My Little Ponies and sealed it down with the Etch-a-Sketch. So that no one could find it to take it back.

They had another row soon after that and Dad went away for five days, the longest he had ever been gone. He came back once and slept on the sofa; she saw the crumpled cushions in the morning and plunged her face into them to inhale his smell. Rosie blamed her mother; she knew that she had driven him away. And when Dad returned he seemed to agree with her.

'I'm sorry, little one,' he said, sitting on the side of her bed. 'But your mother . . . well, she and I . . . we're not the best of friends so I thought I should stay away. I thought we'd get to be friends again if we had a break. You understand?'

'But you're still not friends,' said Rosie.

'No,' he said slowly. 'We aren't.'

'It's *her* fault,' said Rosie, watching his face. 'You're much nicer than her. She's always crying and shouting at me these days.'

A small smile flickered across his face and was gone. He lent across the bed and kissed her cheek. 'It's both of us who are at fault, Rosie. Goodnight.'

But Rosie could tell what he really thought; whose fault it really was.

It was Rosie's birthday in six days. That week, the household was unusually peaceful. Dad came in early nearly every night and the three of them had tea together; her mother cooked all of her favourites – spaghetti on toast, macaroni cheese and fish fingers. When they were alone she treated her differently too, sitting down with her to watch cartoons on TV after school and asking her questions about her friends and her lessons in a soft, low voice that was quite unlike her normal one. Rosie liked the attention but she felt awkward; she would rather have watched alone as she usually did. Dad always brought her presents now too; when she heard him unlock the door she ran to him and he gave her books – difficult ones with no pictures – or crayons or colourful rubbers that didn't work but smelled lovely.

On the night before her birthday there was another row – the worst yet. She heard her mother wailing incoherently, then a crash and smashing china, as though she had hurled a cup across the room. Her voice became louder until she was screaming.

'You promised – you *promised*! You *bastard*, you *swore* to me! Now *this* –' Another crash. 'I'm leaving you and I'm taking my child.'

'You can't take her, you know that. You're a depressive, the courts would give her to me.'

'I will. I will. You can't stop me!'

'Susan.' Dad's voice was calm and gentle. 'What you do, only you can decide. But Rosie – she doesn't even like you. She told me that. She prefers to be with me.'

There was a howling like a wild animal and a scuffling, a thump like a chair falling over. Then only low guttural sobs and the sound of dragging feet coming upstairs. Rosie sat up in bed petrified lest her mother would come in and try to take her away. But the footsteps passed her room and faded down the corridor. She fell into an uneasy sleep.

In the morning, Dad woke her up with his arms full of presents. It was usually her mother who did that.

'Mum's gone out for a while, she'll be back later,' said Dad, reading her thoughts. 'Anyway, I thought you'd rather have me bring in your presents this year.'

So began the most wonderful birthday ever. She opened her presents; a pile of delight topped with a pair of blue and pink rollerblades. Then they had breakfast – chocolate croissants and banana milkshakes and afterwards went to the park to practise rollerblading. Dad held her hand while she tottered along and caught her when she fell. Soon she could skate without holding on and Dad clapped his hands and told her that she was the coolest, most beautiful girl in the park. After a few hours they were both hungry so Dad bought her an ice cream and took her to McDonalds. Her mother never allowed her to go there, or eat ice cream for that matter.

'You'll thank me when you're older,' her mother said. She

said the same thing when she bought her sandals to wear to school instead of trainers. Rosie did not believe her.

Back at home, they watched *Aladdin* on video, another of her presents. Her mother returned in the middle of the film. She rushed over to the sofa where they were sitting.

'Happy birthday, darling!' she cried, her voice unnaturally loud and bright. 'Did you like your rollerblades?'

'Yes, thank you,' said Rosie, not meeting her eyes. But, she thought, they were Dad's present not yours.

'It took me forever to find them. Woolworths only had blue and yellow; in the end I had to go all the way to London. And did you like the stickers? You can put them on your school bag.'

She chattered on but Rosie was watching her father who had paused the video and was fiddling with something in the kitchen. She heard the rustle of cellophane and a match strike. He came back into the room with the most fantastic cake she had ever seen, better even than Richie Evans's football cake that his mother had paid thirty pounds for. It was pink and round and ringed with candles. In its centre was a picture of a girl – herself – in purple piped icing, wearing rollerblades.

'Like it?' asked Dad, smiling but before she had time to reply her mother cut in, her voice icy cold.

'Robert,' she said, spitting out the word. 'You know I've made her a cake.'

'Well I'd forgotten. But she can have two cakes – why not? Bring yours out, don't cause a scene, for Christ's sake.'

Her mother's cake was chocolate as usual; a square of brown sponge with thick gooey icing spilling down the sides. At its centre was a face outlined in smarties with hundreds and thousands for hair and a crown picked out in candles. It looked good but it was homemade and not in any way special.

'I want the pink cake.' Dad set about cutting a big slice.

'I'll have some of yours later,' she said graciously to her mother, catching her eye as she did so. She was looking at her with a strange expression, a look that was so odd it was frightening.

Dad hadn't noticed. 'Blow out the candles then so that I can cut it. And don't forget to make a wish.'

'Silly Dad – I'm seven not eight.'

'Never mind – one for luck.'

She blew out the candles in two puffs, almost in one but the last flame refused to go out. Then she closed her eyes.

'I wish it could always be like today. Just Dad and me and lots of presents.' Then, maliciously, because her mother was listening, 'and *nobody* else.'

When she opened her eyes her mother had left the room.

'That wasn't a terribly nice wish,' said Dad.

'But I love it when it's just you and me; we always have the best time on our own.'

Dad was inexpertly dividing the pink cake into segments. But to Rosie's horror the slice that he placed in front of her was not pink sponge as she expected, but fruit cake.

'Oh, Dad – I hate fruit cake!'

'You eat it at Christmas, don't you?'

'No I don't! Mum makes me special sponge at Christmas. I never eat Christmas cake.'

'Oh well, you'll just have to eat the icing.'

So she picked off the icing. It was dry and tasteless and she looked around for the chocolate cake. It had gone. Later on she found it in the bin. Dad had put teabags on top of it so she couldn't rescue it. What a shame, she thought, and then she remembered her rollerblades and the sweetness of the day returned.

The next day was a Sunday. She usually read in bed on Sundays because Dad liked to sleep in late. Then it occurred to her that he might be sleeping on the sofa again, so she put on her dressing gown to go and look. She was half way down the stairs when the living room door opened and Dad started up towards her.

'Let's wake up Mum,' he said. 'Let's surprise her.'

'Aw, Dad, do we have to?'

'Yes we do, chicken. I've something very important to tell her and I want you there too. Come on.' He took her hand and they went up the stairs together and down the long corridor to the big bedroom. The door was closed and he tried the handle as if he expected it to be locked, but it was open. He opened the door and shut it again almost at once without going inside. Rosie was just behind him and he nearly trod on her as he backed out.

'Go to your room at once and stay there,' he said, his voice shaky.

'Why? What's wrong?'

'DO AS YOU'RE BLOODY TOLD!' He grabbed her hand and dragged her down the landing to her room, shutting the door on her. She heard him run downstairs and two minutes later, run back up and charge down the corridor. When she heard his footsteps returning, slowly this time, she opened the door.

'What's wrong with Mum?'

He did not answer but walked past her as though she were invisible, his head sunk on his chest.

Next thing the house was full of people. An ambulance arrived and two policewomen. One of them took Rosie downstairs and asked to see her toys. They watched a bit of *Aladdin* together but all the time the phone was ringing and the doorbell jangling and the woman would not tell her what was happening or let her go and look. When she finally set her free everyone had gone except for the other policewoman and a blonde woman with red nails and lips who kissed Rosie and had kissed Dad, for she could see the red imprint on his cheek.

Rosie asked, 'What's the matter with Mum?' No one answered; the women looked at Dad but he said nothing. Rosie wasn't excited anymore. She was horribly, terribly scared. There was a deep pain in her stomach and she thought she might be sick.

'What's the matter with Mum?' she cried.

'She's gone away for a while, darling,' said the policewoman.

'I don't care what you say,' cried Rosie, but she knew that her mother was dead. Dead! Dead is forever. How could she not see her mother ever again? How could this happen?

She remembered her birthday wish.

'Did she die because I wished that she wouldn't be here?'

'No, sweetheart,' said Dad at last but his eyes were lying and when he put his arms around her and cried into her neck his smell was different, as though the lie had seeped into his body and soured his skin.

LAVERBREAD

~

Liz Hinds

According to the police report, the weather on the day of the accident was bright and sunny. It hadn't rained for five days and the ground was dry. I've gone and called it an accident. Sorry, that was a slip of the tongue. The coroner has not yet pronounced his judgement and until he does, it is an incident not an accident, the police say. But of course it was an accident. My Mum loved us too much for it to have been anything else.

I love the smell of the sea. I can smell it in the house sometimes when the wind is in the right direction, and then I open all the windows to let it in, but out here, coming straight off the water, it's sweeter, untainted by town odours. And sweetest because it carries with it so many memories. When I was a little girl Mammy would take me with her to gather cockles. In those days we didn't know about the pollution in the bay, all the chemicals from the industry in the valley that nobody bothered to clean up but poured straight down the Tawe into our lovely bay. The poison and the shit, we didn't know about any of that. We took the sea for granted, it was just there. It was where we learnt to swim, me and John, off the steps out along the prom. Mammy would sit at the top and watch us, and when we'd had enough, when our teeth were chattering so much neither of us could stand it any more, and we'd have to give in, she'd wrap us both in big stripey towels she kept just for summer and swimming, and she'd rub us down till we shouted to her to stop, we're warm now, Mammy.

But you could only swim in the bay when the tide was in. When it's out, it's a mile at least to get to it through squelchy mud. Like melted chocolate, mud that slurps around your toes and sucks you into itself. We didn't walk on it if we could help it except when we went with Mammy to collect cockles. Then we all, Mammy and John and me, wore wellies to protect us against whatever was lurking there. We never saw anything, but we knew there were things below the surface just waiting for our feet.

You've got to follow the tide out if you want to collect cockles. Mammy liked to go in the early mornings, when the sun was light and clear, and the air was salty fresh. She would carry the rake and bucket and John and me would skip from puddle to puddle, spotting crabs and tiny shrimps. By the time you got all the way out to the best cockle beds, you couldn't hear a sound; the village and its life and noise could have been a million miles away, not just across the sandbanks. We wouldn't be alone, there were always a few people out there gathering cockles, and they'd say, 'There's a good bed here, come and join us,' and we'd go over and then the hard work would start.

Mammy would rake the sand and John and me would collect up the cockles and put them in our bucket. 'Not that one,' Mammy would say sometimes, 'that one's too small, leave it time to grow up a bit, take its big sister instead.' Or, 'That's an ugly old one, all open like that, we don't want his sort.' Then, when our bucket was full, we'd carry it between us over to the nearest puddle and we'd rinse them to get rid of as much sand as we could, before carrying them all the way back home. We'd take it in turns. Mammy would carry the bucket for a bit and then John and me would struggle with the narrow metal handle digging into our palms. Mammy made up a game for us to play as we trekked back shorewards. We'd look at the village and spot people's houses and try and guess what they were doing right at that moment. 'Mr Rees, he'll have been out for hours with the fishing boat and Mrs Rees will be washing the children's clothes. Imagine having seven children to wash for,' Mammy would say.

'Poor Mrs Rees. And old Mrs Evans will be sitting at her window waiting for her son to come back from the war.'

'Can you see her? Cooee, Mrs Evans.'

'Don't be daft, John, she can't hear you.'

'I know that, she wouldn't hear the foghorn if it was in her front room. And there's Mrs Penry's house, la di da, bet she's still in bed, waiting for her maid to bring her breakfast, yes ma'am, no ma'am, thank you ma'am.'

Then when we got home, the old tin bath would be out ready in the back-yard. Daddy would have got it out from the shed. Not the best bath, the one we use on Sunday night, but the one that leaks and can't go inside, and we'd set to, fetching jugs of water from the outside tap to wash the cockles. Mammy would wash them until she was sure they were clean. Not a grain of sand would be found in those shells once Mammy had finished with them, then she'd take them into the scullery and we could go and play, until she called us to come and eat them. The sweetest mouthfuls ever to come out of the sand and all the better for the work we'd had to do getting them. With crispy fried best bacon, it had to be best, Mammy only ever bought the best food. She knew how to look after her family.

There were three witnesses, who all said different things. The first one, a man out walking his dog, said he'd seen Mum walking close to the cliffs. He thought she might be a visitor who didn't know the area and he'd called out to her to take care. The cliffs could be unstable near the edge. But she didn't appear to hear him. He didn't see her fall. The other witnesses were two women who'd been taking a stroll before going for coffee and were busy chatting when they noticed Mum. The first one said she'd seen a woman walking very close to the edge but hadn't seen her fall. The other one said she got the impression that the woman had walked straight at the edge. The coroner asked her how sure she was, if she would swear to that. She said she was sure but she couldn't swear to it. So that means she wasn't really sure at all, doesn't it? It stands to reason. There was no reason why Mum would have walked at the edge.

Every Sunday Mammy made us a big roast dinner. Sometimes a rosy joint of beef, with Yorkshire pudding and mashed potatoes and swede and cabbage and thick rich brown gravy, shiny with beef fat, which we mopped up with chunks of bread. But Daddy's favourite, and mine too, was roast lamb. Mammy would cook it till it was just right, tender and still full of juice and taste. Sometimes we went to Auntie Mary's for Sunday dinner and she always cooked lamb because she knew it was Daddy's favourite but when she cooked it, it was tough and tasted of nothing, not at all like Mammy's. When we had lamb for Sunday dinner it was my job to make the mint sauce. Daddy grew mint in the garden, or it grew itself. 'This blooming mint,' he'd grumble, 'it gets everywhere.' Just before Sunday dinnertime I'd go out and pick a handful of the freshest greenest looking leaves and take them into the scullery. There I had to strip the leaves off the stalks and wrap them up together before tearing them into tiny bits. The leaves had to be torn not cut to keep their flavour, Mammy said, then into Mammy's little crystal glass jug they'd go with some vinegar and a drop of hot water and a pinch of sugar, and I'd stir it, till it was all mixed up, and then I'd put the jug on its own special saucer and take it to the table. And when we'd eaten dinner Daddy would say, 'This is fine lamb, Megan, love, but tell me who made this wonderful mint sauce?'

And I'd say, 'Me, Daddy, it was me.'

And he'd say, 'Well, who'd have thought it, I can tell you're going to a great cook just like your Mammy.' And that was all I ever wanted to be. Just like my Mammy.

Doctor Lloyd spoke at the inquest today. He's not the doctor who saw her after she fell but her own doctor. He said Mum'd been suffering with depression and he'd prescribed anti-depressants. I didn't know. I looked at Dad, expecting him to look shocked but he just sat there staring straight ahead. Then Doctor Lloyd said, 'Mrs Williams was depressed following the death of her mother.' Of course she was depressed. Anyone would be if they'd just lost their mother. That doesn't mean it wasn't an accident.

When the court adjourned for lunch, I asked Dad if he'd known she'd seen the doctor. He said he hadn't, but he'd found the prescription in her handbag after she died. Mum didn't like taking pills but she wasn't stupid, she would have taken them if she'd thought she needed them, if she was really depressed.

Mammy always knew how to take care of us. She was never still, always cleaning or ironing, shopping or washing. I'd watch her standing at the sink in the scullery in her flowery wrap-round pinny over her short-sleeved blouse, scrubbing clothes. She had strong arms and her knuckles were always red but her touch was gentle. Sometimes she'd straighten up and wipe her hand across her forehead and spot me out of the corner of her eye. 'You gave me a fright,' she'd say. 'Haven't you got anything to do?' and I'd shake my head and she'd say, 'Come on then, you can put these through the mangle for me.' I loved to use the mangle, even though it took all of my might to turn the big iron handle as Mammy fed the sheets through until every drop of water was squeezed out. 'There's a good girl,' she'd say, 'helping your Mammy, now, you take those corners, don't let them drop on the floor, and we'll hang them out to blow, it's a good drying day today.' And when we'd pegged all the sheets on the line, she'd pull the string to raise it so the sheets were as high as the bedroom windows and they'd fill out with gusts like sailing boats on the sea-sky. Then Mammy would go and put the kettle on, because a nice cup of tea was just what she needed.

It was always warm in the scullery, with the oven on, with a stew slow cooking or cakes baking, boiled cake or teisen lap, and, once a week, mammy made a batch of my favourite welshcakes. She'd get the griddle out, she had to do that, I wasn't strong enough to lift it, and she'd put it on the stove to heat up while she was making the mixture, rubbing in the flour and the butter, only the best Welsh butter will do, got to give them the right flavour, and stirring in the currants and the sugar and the egg. She never weighed things out, she knew what she needed more of or when there was enough, and then she'd let me roll it out, not too thin mind, and between us we'd cut out the circles of sweet dough. The first cut was the best, before the leftovers were kneaded together again and again until we were left with a piece the size of half a crown. But she cooked every bit of it, nothing was wasted, standing over the griddle, watching and waiting and turning. And I'd run in and out of the kitchen saying, 'Are they ready yet, Mammy?'

And Mammy would say, 'Wait a minute, lovely girl, you can't hurry them or they burn on the outside and they're raw on the inside,' and I would go away again and count to a hundred before letting myself go back in. And at last my patience would be rewarded and I'd get there just as Mammy was putting the first ones on the tray to cool, and I'd breathe in and heaven must smell like hot welshcakes straight off the griddle. Then Mammy would say, 'Go on then, you can choose one as you were such a help to me to make them,' and I'd stare at them hard until I'd decided which one was the most perfect and then I'd take it, carefully because it was still hot, 'Take a plate you daft thing,' and I'd go and sit on a chair because I needed to be sitting down to enjoy this properly. Even when I was sitting down, I made myself wait for my first mouthful. I wanted it to last forever. I can taste it now, warm and sweet and reminding me of Mammy.

Dad had to give evidence at the inquest this afternoon. The coroner asked him about his 'wife's state of mind'. What was he supposed to say? Yes, she'd been sad since her mother had died, of course she had. Dad admitted that she'd been upset ever since Gran had first gone into a home. Mum knew it was for the best but she still felt she should be the one to look after Gran. 'They don't look after Mammy right in that place,' she'd say. 'They don't know what Mammy likes.' She always called Gran Mammy. I hated it. Hated the Welshness. Was embarrassed by the little girl-ness. We all told Mum it was impossible for us to have Gran to stay. We were all out at work all day. Gran needed someone with her all the time. Mostly she was fine but you never knew when she was going to take it into her head to do something daft. Like the time she caught the bus to the train station. She was thinking Gramps was still alive and he'd gone to drive his train without taking any sandwiches. So she made some and took them up for him. The station-master phoned Mum and said she'd better come and get her mother. Mum said wasn't that just like Mammy, always looking after others. Mum talked about giving up her job to look after her but Dad wasn't keen. Didn't want Gran living in the house with us, I suppose. But that's like

Mum too, always looking after people. She'd been upset about Gran but not crazy upset. I mean, she wasn't acting strangely or anything. She wouldn't do anything to hurt us.

I've always been a coward, cowardy cowardy custard. If I grazed my knee or bruised my elbow I'd cry buckets. When I was little, sometimes, not very often but now and again, Mammy would take us to gather seaweed. Daddy loved laverbread tossed in oatmeal and fried in bacon fat. John and I hated it but Mammy and Daddy would eat it with cockles and bacon. Usually Mammy would buy it from the market in town but sometimes she'd be in the mood to go and gather it. That meant another long walk, this time over the rocks. 'Careful,' Mammy would say, 'that seaweed is slippery,' and I was never as fast as John and I would fall as I tried to keep up with him. Mammy'd come over to me as I sat on the rock, holding my bleeding knee, tears running down my face, and she'd cooch me to her, and John would be shouting, 'Cissy, crying over a little scratch.'

'Hush you, here let Mammy kiss it better,' and she'd splash sea water over it which made it sting, and she'd wipe it with her handkerchief and say, 'There all better now,' and it was her love that made it so.

And whenever she cooked laverbread, she always said, 'Go on, just have a bit, you might like it,' but I'd tried it lots of times and it's horrid, all black and slimy and urgh. Mammy loves it though. I wonder if she'd like some now. I could get some, she could have it for her lunch. They don't feed her properly in that place. She doesn't look well. They're not looking after her right. But laverbread is good for you, Mammy said, it's rich in iron, good for your blood, I could help make her better just like she always made me better. We used to come out here to collect it, just over there, where the rocks are being uncovered now as the tide goes out. That's where we always used to collect it, I'm sure. But I don't remember where the path down is. It must be here somewhere. Oh, why can't I find it? Mammy would know where it was if she was here. I'll never be like Mammy.

'I've listened to what everyone has said. And you're all wrong. My mother was sad when my gran died but she wasn't crazy. My mother would never have killed herself. She knew the cliffs well. She'd walked there since she was a child. She was probably looking at a flower – she loved the flowers on the cliff path – and got too close to the edge. We all loved her. We'd have noticed if something was wrong. We got on well, she'd have talked to me. She'd have told me, if there'd been anything wrong. Every night when I got home from work, I told her all about my day and she, well, she always listened to me. She'd have told me. And I'd have helped her.'

I'll find it, Mammy. Just as you like it. I'm coming.

THE WOMAN WHO LOVED CUCUMBERS

~

Gillian Brightmore

She placed them in her fridge: cool, dark and slender. She surrounded them with her fingers, testing their firmness. Yes, later she would take one out, carefully, and then she would bite and crunch until the juice oozed out into her mouth and slipped down her throat. She liked them raw and unpeeled. Sometimes she could eat two or three a day quite easily, consuming so much that at her local shops she became known as 'the cucumber lady'. She had begun to buy from two or three different places so as not to cause too much comment, but her craving was such that if she did not call in every few days for her cucumbers people remarked on her absence. She had recently been away on holiday for a week, at a hotel, and her desire had become so strong that she had been forced to buy one and keep it in her room, to eat in secret. They had been served in salads, with tomatoes and lettuce, but once sliced they were of no interest to her.

Often, when she went to answer the phone, her mouth would be filled with cucumber. Her friends imagined that she was having a snack, but no, she was chewing and savouring their rich succulence. When her men friends called she especially liked to have a cucumber, to hand as it were, and to take a quick bite. Only once had anyone remarked upon the smell of her breath.

She kept them from her children, afraid that they would notice her growing obsession, and that they would eat too much of her supply. She rationed them to thin slices! She dreaded a dock strike, a vegetable shortage. She didn't dream of them at night, no, not yet. Could there be any harm in her craving? she sometimes idly wondered. Once she thought she had remembered reading of a woman who turned orange as a result of eating too many carrots.

By night, when the wind howled around the house, then she sometimes grew afraid, while the cucumbers lay ice cold in the fridge below.

Her friends did not take her addiction seriously. They dismissed it as an eccentricity due to the loss of her much-loved husband. When she tentatively mentioned it to her doctor he seemed unconcerned and merely said she had been a widow too long. Occasionally, as her longing persisted, she wondered whether she should see a psychiatrist, now that everything in her life seemed to be dominated and controlled by this obsessive need, the overwhelming desire for cool, green flesh, for the colour of greenness. Was it substitution of some subtle kind? Did she need replacement therapy? The primal scream technique? Her mind reeled.

Did she yearn for more carnal pleasures? The thought of sex seemed remote to her now and she never allowed a complete relationship. But there was always this longing, always. She could not describe their hold over her, the power to which she was now in thrall: their aroma, the bite and then the crunch. A Canadian friend wondered whether she had considered rather more exotic vegetables: squash, pumpkin or avocado? But neither their colours nor their shapes attracted her and besides they just did not have that bite! And so she settled down with her predilection.

At times the longing totally overcame her. She was powerless against it. She was unable to continue without handling, touching and then biting that firm greenness. Would she continue, she wondered, to live on like that as though she were some fairy queen lying alone with her strange desire? She shivered.

As the summer came she wondered whether she should begin to grow them: cucumbers. She could even develop her own strain. The idea appealed to her even though she had no gardening skills. There were two old greenhouses in her garden that could be used. She imagined filling these glass houses with their dazzling profusion, her cucumbers. She did not question whether such a complex feat might be beyond her, but began. She bought propagators and began to nurture the seeds.

In spite of her lack of gardening knowledge the plants began to thrive. It seemed to her she had green fingers. Perhaps it was because of the intensity of her interest and the care that she lavished on them that they flourished so well. She meticulously noted their growth and their watering was carefully regulated. She learned from experience just how much water was enough and when it was too much. The cucumbers became like babies, so much so that at times she imagined that she could hear them breathe.

She loved to sit in one of her greenhouses surrounded by her plants, especially when it was sunny and their leaves and fruits glistened and shone in the sun and a delicate aroma arose in the air like an elixir. It was then she realised that they were always in her mind.

So her life, consumed by this desire, passed. Suddenly it seemed to her that the nights grew colder and the daylight shortened ominously. She began to fear for their survival. The cucumbers, to her eyes, grew pale. She had to make the decision to bring them indoors. She had a small side room that would suit, airy and with plenty of light. When they were settled in and growing well she decided to move a few upstairs to another sunny room. And so it began. It was a relentless progress. They advanced through the house.

When her friends called unexpectedly she had to close more and more doors behind her. She would say, 'Oh, that room's in such a mess!' and would deftly close the door with a laugh.

Her friends began to eye her a little strangely and to comment and mutter among themselves. Some began to stay away.

More and more rooms began to be taken over by them, so much so her cats became afraid when they prowled through the house at night. She sent her children away to relatives for a while so that she was free to concentrate on her cucumbers. They did not return. She rejected love; she rejected reality. She sought her only solace in her cucumbers and so her double life began.

She struggled in vain to control their advance through her home as well as her obsession with them. Quite often, at night, late and alone, she would sneak around the house for a last look, a last bite.

But she slept uneasily and dreamed. The dreams became nightmares; the cucumbers were marching down her wide white staircase, majestic in their arrogance, green on white. She lay, stretched out at the foot of the staircase, a fine jade necklace around her throat and her legs and arms tinged with a greenish hue as though some final process had taken place. She awoke shuddering, her forehead damp. What kind of betrayal was this?

After all, she thought later that morning, there was no harm in what she did although yet another friend remarked that he could smell cucumbers on her breath, as though he had been speaking of an alcoholic. But the longing still overcame her reason. She could now never pass a cucumber without a shiver, a thrill of exhilaration tinged, now, with fear that ran through her like a sudden chill. The cucumbers were as firmly rooted in her mind as though they had been planted there.

She realised one morning that she had developed a new strain, a more radical type of cucumber, particularly succulent, even sweet. It exactly suited her taste, dark olive green, glossy and, she felt, svelte. She was elated. She had succeeded in growing them and they were flourishing in her home. Their existence became her raison d'être. She felt that she had met with ecstasy. She sat like an Empress, a queen among cucumbers, content in her rituals.

She went out less and less. There was no need, all that she required was here, surrounding her. She spoke less and less, except to the cucumbers. She had never spoken of them to her friends, fearing in some strange way to betray her fruits! She saw the world pass outside her windows, but she had no part in it. Other people were experiencing joy, pain, growth or emotion but she was incarcerated alone, anaesthetized behind closed doors where she was surrounded by cucumber seas. She took another bite.

She was at peace now and there was no night too long to count all her cucumbers.

Another summer came, hot and heady. She opened all her windows. The growth of the cucumbers accelerated, their colour sharpened, and she felt dizzy in their presence. As the summer passed, growing hotter and drier, behind her elation grew into a sneaking unease, an anxiety.

She could not put a name to it. She began to water and fertilise her plants excessively, suddenly fearing that they might thirst or hunger. She dared not go away on holiday or visit her children, and leave the cucumbers alone. They consumed all her thoughts. Her children, when they briefly returned, became small figures flitting in and out between the cucumber plants. She herself became light-headed and was continually anxious. Her doctor prescribed tranquillizers.

The nurturing and love of her cucumbers had now became all of her life. She felt she had no choice. She was resigned to serve them even though the years might close in around her. She was held in thrall. This was her destiny, her fate; her body honed and tuned to this ethic of desire that had no mercy. Only occasionally did she worry that she was neglecting everything else in her life and that the world had become a shadow.

Friends hardly ever called on her now. She sensed that they were uncomfortable with her distracted conversation and her wild-eyed anxiety. It was as though she imagined that a cucumber might at any moment burst upon them, having suddenly developed now powers. She sighed. Sometimes she wept. The cucumbers went on flourishing quietly, clustering secretly around their stalks.

Of course she did not altogether trust them. That, she supposed, was the price of adoration. Now she dreamed of them continually. Indeed, at times it was difficult to distinguish dream from reality. Sometimes she found herself wondering what other people did, without cucumbers. She played with their colour and wove them into her moods. They always awaited her presence. From the outside her house might have seemed like a prison, but to her it was a sanctuary, a temple, a place of worship. For the first time she felt there was something a little sinister about them, their greenery like armour, even arrogance.

She began to have headaches. On some days she fancied her flesh had a greenish hue and felt clammy to the touch. She knew that she was awaiting some final overthrow, some awful power struggle. Outside, the sun filtered down through the trees like lace. Inside, the doors creaked behind her as she closed them upon her cucumbers, where they lay leafing in their sea of green. Then the horror of her obsession finally penetrated and overcome her. It was as though all the clocks in the city had been stranded at midnight.

When the morning came the day was filled with brilliance and daffodils stood yellow in tubs on the terraces throughout the city below. But she could hardly see for the skeins of greenness drifting before her eyes, clouding her vision. She knew now she must rise up and displace them from her heart, dislodge those irresistible longings, take action, and eliminate them, savagely and with decisiveness. But it would not be easy.

She walked into the kitchen. She selected the sharpest of her kitchen knives and then sharpened it again. She walked slowly into her garden. She knelt before them. It was her final homage. They lay basking in the hot spring sun, luxuriating in the flooding light, abandoned in greenness. She knew now that she had become part of them.

No doubt they believed she had been overcome.

She put down the knife. What would she do afterwards, in those long hours that lay ahead of her without this thrall, this desire? How could her life be emptied of this overwhelming compulsion? What would become of her? She picked up the knife. She began to cut at the roots. They turned towards her in their cool scorn and supreme egotism, these things that she had loved. Then they lay waste around her. She destroyed her desire and the consuming tyranny of their flesh.

The green hue left the sky. She knew that she would see the sun again. She stood up and faced the sky. The light fell around her like a benediction. She could not look down. Her limbs, that had been heavy in their cocoon of bondage, lightened. She had met with ecstasy. But she had overcome her green desire.

She was out of confinement for the first time.

RETREAT

~

Alexandra Ward

I knew as soon as I got there, I'd made the wrong choice. It was late afternoon. Raining, sort of. A miserable drizzle on the point of resolving itself into cloud and rolling off down the valley. The single-decker bus off-loaded me at the start of a rutted track gouged out of moorland. The only hint of colour came from the rust, orange and eau-de-nil lichens, that adhered like crushed sea anemones to the stone posts that signified its start. The sagging dripping fence-wire swung from rotted post to post like scalloped ratlines on a ghostly shroud, and the oily pools reflected an afterglow, almost an absence, of light. Inviting, it was not.

Fortunately, I had been advised to 'travel light' – a change of casual clothes, a weather-proof jacket, fleece. A light-weight backpack. I hoisted the latter on my shoulders and set off up the track. A mile-and-a-half on, having curved and climbed, the track dipped suddenly and precipitately, making for a low huddle of stone buildings in the hollow below. A bedraggled feather of smoke hung down across the slate roof of the main building, promising fire. But there was no other sign of life. No door burst open in friendly greeting. No one looked out from the small deep-set windows, and I hesitated to peer in. Averting my gaze as I passed one piggy-eyed aperture, I knocked on the damp yet dessicated door. I could hear a low murmur but it stopped at my first rap. The door remained closed to me. I see, I thought, only self-starters need apply. I turned the big white china handle and walked in. The room was long, low ceilinged, stone-flagged and ill-lit, despite numerous small night-lights that were dotted about. In the gloom, I could make out several people silently and separately engaged in various tasks. A man down on his knees before the huge open hearth trying to coax a weakling fire from damp wood. A woman chopping raw vegetables at one end of a huge wooden table. A woman stacking wooden bowls and cutlery at the other end of the table. Others sitting, each before his or her own night-light, their faces impassive, almost smug, in the dim glow. No one looked up as I entered, no one said anything.

Indeed, no one chose to mark my coming in any way whatever. They might have been a tableau-not-so-vivant at a Folk Museum. An impression enhanced by the fact that they were all dressed in variations of designer grunge and born-again Celt. My Ramblers' Anonymous seemed very down market.

I had been informed that silence was entirely optional at this retreat. I should not have come otherwise. I had no wish to be chastised for infringements of a strict rule. While I might court a little temporary peace, I knew I should not be able to sustain it for a whole weekend. However, I had not expected everyone to exercise their right to silence the minute I appeared. I'd been the new kid on the block many times before and it always got up my nose. Now, standing just inside the threshold, I wondered whether the done thing would be to announce myself. 'Hi! I'm Linda. I'm 43. Divorced. No children. A computer operator, from Cardiff, and I'm happy to be able to share with you.'

Before I was tempted to make an ass of myself, a man came over to me and, without a word, took both my hands in his, and still holding me by one hand (which sent warning bells jangling about hangovers from seventies grope-groups) led me back through a door, out through what looked and smelt like some forgotten corner in a copyright library's bookstacks, and up a narrow, twisted, abysmally dark stairs. This opened immediately into a room taking up the entire roof space. The bare boards were almost hidden under neat rows of bed rolls and sleeping bags. At the head of each cocoon-like mound was a biscuit tin with one of those ubiquitous night-lights. The leaflet had said 'spartan'. I'd imagined a solitary cell of aesthetic minimalism, white as the heart of a lily, and with a gothic aperture of some sort through which an ivy tendril wound its exploratory way. (I have read *Northanger Abbey* and I should have known better.)

By way of explanation, my companion said, 'We are hoping to convert the outhouses eventually.' Ah ha! The in-crowd downstairs has decided to let the punters (moi) in to pay for the improvements. I quashed the thought. After all, retreats are supposed to ground you, reintegrate you. It wouldn't do to cultivate my natural bitterness. Spartan. My idea of spartan had included white linen on firm beds, and, at worst, tepid showers and abrasive towels in natural undyed fibres. Spartan, I could handle. There was no sign of 'a bathroom' or 'The Bathroom'. A spade by the front door took on a sinister significance. I felt tired, dirty, hungry and depressed. My spirits sank as low as they could go. Was I about to enter The Dark Night of the Soul?

I turned to my companion. 'I'm the Facilitator,' he said, but did not offer his hand this time, so that my right hand made a funny jerking movement all on its own, so well trained in the customary civilities. 'Our leaflet. It explains everything.'

'Yes,' I said, quickly recounting its ten commandments that had seemed so appealing but which now had a peni-tential ring:

1. *One need not speak.*
2. *One should move slowly.*
3. *Meditate on the hour every hour.*
4. *Travel light.*
5. *Find your task.*
6. *Cleanse your soul.*
7. *Bow your head.*
8. *Bear your load.*
9. *Pull your weight.*
10. *Leave in peace.*

'Right then. It's up to you.' He turned and whizzed down the dark well of the stairs, and I made a mental note that the rules must be for the punters only.

I looked down at the thin orange-and-chocolate flowered sleeping-bag, and hoped there would be 'Joy through suffering', as suffer I surely would. There was no escape. I took out my winceyette pyjamas and tucked them under the purple nylon pillow. I hung my backpack from the shaker peg rail that ran the full length of the room on either side. The other pegs were hung with backpacks and towels giving the room the appearance of Bluebeard's secret room of corpses. There were no outer garments, so I slipped off my jacket, and took it downstairs. Again, I heard the low murmur as I approached the kitchen door.

Everyone was as I had left them, chopping, fire-raising, meditating, and, surprise surprise, silent. I put my jacket with the others hanging from another Shaker rail by the door, and went over to Chopping Woman. 'May I help?' my voice squeaked. She didn't look at me, just shook her head. Sod you, I thought, and then remembered I was probably being disciplined into silence for my own good. So I looked about for somewhere to sit and to think about what to do next, as it did not look as if anyone was going to tell me. It was after five, I guess, almost dark outside, and very dark inside, save for the meditating glow-worms.

Apart from Chopping Woman's table and accompanying kitchen chairs, there were three large old sofas, off a skip or the local dump. I went and sat on the empty shiny black one. Big mistake. It made a soughing sound as I did so. No one laughed. There's self-control for you. I should have gone for the uncut moquette with the cigarette-burn pattern and the real cigarette burns, but I would have joggled its passive, focussed, meditating occupant into acknowledging and moving up for me. I didn't have a night-light to stare at, so I looked at the bare third finger on my left hand. It had a ghost ring on it from last summer, our last summer. It felt naked without its small gold shackle.

After what seemed like eons, the chopping stopped, the bowls were spread out and the others sat at the table. There were twelve in all, including the Facilitator. There did not appear to be a place for me. But the Mad Hatter, sorry, the Facilitator, did his bit and facilitated a small space for me at one corner. He did his 'I wanna hold your hand' act and drew me to it. After that, I was on my own again. Coleslaw (cut rugged), cottage cheese (slightly off), wholemeal bread (slightly mouldy), yoghurt (slightly watery), and honey (blended and of unknown origin). I chewed and chewed. It was fortunate that I did not have to make polite conversation after all.

I took a quick shifty look at everyone – Fire Man, Chopping Woman, the Facilitator, etc. Their heads were bent over their bowls. Their movements were slow and studied, almost a kind of table tai chi. I slowed down so as not to finish before everyone and then speeded up again so as not to be last. It was worse than being married.

The meal accomplished, everyone got up, passing their bowls and cutlery to me as they did so. I guess that makes me Washing-up Woman. (I'd thought we were to 'find our own roles'. Wrong again.) Trying to 'bear my load' and 'pull my weight' I stacked them neatly then looked about for a sink, taps, the usual things. I opened doors which turned out to be cupboards and cupboards which turned out to be doors. Nothing. There was a worn red plastic bowl on a windowsill, but no sign of taps from which to fill it. I opened the backdoor to look for a pump. The utter blackness was suffocating. I stumbled back inside as if for air. No one paid any attention. They were all looking at their little night-lights now, so I couldn't interrupt them. They were quite safe.

I crawled upstairs on my hands and knees and 'more by luck than judgement' located my pallet and my own precious little light and matches. I lit up and sat on the bed and meditated. Why the hell had I come here? How the hell could I get out? But I was too tired and too dispirited to keep it up for long. Still fully clothed, I crawled inside my bag, and with the faint smell of boiled cabbage and new lime wash in my nose, fell asleep. After what seemed like a moment, I started awake. It was still deeply dark, but I was aware that there were others, prone and supine, in the room. My stomach was grossly distended from all the roughly chopped roughage. I cursed Chopping Woman, and, surruptitiously, slowly and silently expelled the painful noxious gases. Every time I thought I'd got to the last of it, a new balloon-full built up. I could stand it no longer. I had to get up and out for fear that the whole room would be discovered in the morning gassed and neatly laid out in its bags like a cult mass suicide.

There were already three little glow-worm lights burning when I lumbered into the kitchen. No fire, no food, just dis-embodied faces staring at tiny lights. Two men and a woman, as far one from another as it was possible to be, and totally self-absorbed. On the table, just as I'd left them, were the dirty dishes from the night before. Ignoring the three wise monkeys, I picked out the mug I'd used and rooted around for a kettle, a stove, a primus, anything. Nothing.

It was still too dark to do a thorough search. I sat at the table, head in hands, to wait for dawn. She was a long time coming. I rested my head on my arms, closed my eyes, and, like a child, felt that by doing so I had temporarily disappeared from view. It must have worked. One of the monkeys got up from his rather sloppy lotus position and began getting things together for a hot drink of sorts. I couldn't see from where he'd got the kettle. The other two joined him at the far end of the table. They sat and sipped their drinks savouring every drop. No one attempted to wake me, to include me in. So I began a rather hammy waking scene, but ditched it as soon as I realised no one was paying any attention. I got up and went over to where all the precious gear was waiting. I knew what to do now. But the kettle was empty.

Right, I thought, mentally pushing against the oppressive silence, which like the darkness, seemed to fill every space and threaten to engulf me. I went over to their end of the table. And, since no one paid the slightest notice, declaimed to the room at large, 'I need to know where I can find water.' No one moved or spoke. The silence reformed. Solid. Right, I thought again, I'll find it myself, even if it means getting lost on the mountain. I went out of the back door.

They say it's always darkest before the dawn. Dawn was definitely imminent. I couldn't see a bloody thing. If I die out here, I thought, it will be in all the papers. You'll be rooted out like a rat's nest. So much then for your nice little earner.

I stayed just outside the door for a face-saving interval,

then went back inside. The monkeys were in meditation mode again. I sat on the uncut moquette waiting for the Facilitator to come and live up to his name, and meditated on the tiny, deeply recessed window opposite. I watched its absolute blackness ever so slowly leach away. Dawn dawned at some indefinable point. By which time I was locked into position and could have stayed put for all eternity. They were all up now and moving about the room as if they were enclosed in the fluid of a giant lava lamp, a sort of slow motion mime. Very irritating.

I got up too quickly for someone who had been sitting for so long, and again, to no one in particular, everyone present, like throwing a message in a bottle into a cruel indifferent sea, said, 'I need water if I am to do anything useful.' The Facilitator loomed out of the gloom, took my hand, led me out of the front door. Hey hey, people will talk, I thought, vaguely wondering if he were a reject from the touchy-feely or the happy-clappy school of thought. Still holding my hand, he led the way round the back of the house and down to the brook. It was fairly belting along. A lone bird cued, 'Water, water,' or was it, 'Waster, waster,' from a lone tree. I wondered how many 'retreaties' had disappeared into it, sacrificed, suicidal or just plain lost. Quite a few, I should have thought. There was a bucket and a scoop.

'You do see, don't you, that you must make your own way from here?' he said, abruptly dropping my hand. A human voice, albeit curt, judgmental. Directed at me. I wanted to go down on my knees, beg forgiveness, offer my life. But too late. He was already on his way back up to the house. My mood swung. Don't put yourself out, I thought, pouring icy water into the bucket, and through the eyelets of my boots. The fluorescent strip of light grew broader in the east, accentuating the darkness in the west. It was the perfect moment to overdose on melancholia.

Back inside I found the double-burner camping stove still
out and put the water on to boil. I was thirsty and dirty and
the dishes were waiting. Which came first, in the scheme of
things? I mused, as the water began to get excited. As far as
I could tell, everyone was now down and everyone was
waiting, each little glow-worm alight but no one really concentrating. No sign that they marked my re-entrance though.
Oh what a beautiful morning.

The kettle, which had lost its whistle (or it had been
destroyed for breaking the sacred silence), reached the point
of spitting ferociously. Before I could get to it, Chopping
Woman took it off the burner and passed it to Facilitator Man
who poured its contents into the red plastic bowl and adding
a little cold water from my bucket, proceeded to give himself
a soapless wash.

I stood immobilised, amazed. There he was daintily patting
himself dry on a fragment of old white towel. I couldn't
believe it. It was a reprise of the kettle incident only this time
it was I who was in danger of boiling over. I controlled
myself. 'That was mine,' I said clearly and calmly. Facilitator
Man ignored me, and stood back for Chopping Woman to
take a quick splash. It was intolerable. I looked at the others.
They were concentrating hard on their night-lights. Waiting
for their place in the pecking order. And, suddenly, it clicked.
I'd been here before. Someone trying to teach me a lesson
by oblique means. Power games and punishments. It was
all horribly familiar. I didn't need it anymore. Making as
much noise as possible I banged my way upstairs and into
the fuggy dormitory.

The sound of silence, equally familiar, wafted up to me
from below. Not speaking. Sulking. Ignoring. Every variation
on a theme. I'd had years of it. I stuffed my things into my
backpack, including the night-light (I'd paid for it). All the

time I was doing this I could feel my temper coming to the boil again, building, building. Downstairs Fire Man was busy with his ablutions. Apart from him, no one moved a muscle as I entered the room. The night-lights guttered as I sped across the floor, making for the front door. I opened it. Still no one took any notice. I slammed it. Then I went back to the table. My dirty dishes were still stacked and waiting. I shoved the whole damn lot on the floor. I had their attention at last. Mad Axewoman. I'd 'found my role'.

'Pretentious prats,' I said, back at the door, putting on my jacket. Then, remembering my 'Alice', I yelled as loudly as I could, 'You're nothing but a pack of cards,' felt for the doorknob behind me and backed out, putting paid to the final commandment.

No one came after me. I heard nothing as I went up the path. I imagined fragments of comment: 'couldn't hack it', 'flakey', 'failure to understand first principles'. But I didn't care. I'd had fifteen years of meaningful silence already – moody silence, angry silence, hurt silence, sulky silence. Followed by critical analysis. So what.

I didn't climb back up that track. I flew on winged heels. The air was sweet. The dewy hills tinged pink. The grasses twinkling with beaded webs. I felt like dancing and singing and jumping up and down, but once on the main road, settled for running down each hill as it was surmounted. At the top of one such hill, I was reminded of the fourth commandment and sent my night-light winging in the general direction of some startled sheep. The sense of relief was out of all proportion to the displaced weight.

It was an hour and a half before anyone came along the road behind me. A landrover with a ewe in the back. A farm hand was taking her into the vets in Aber. He dropped me off outside the station, just in time to pick up the Trawscambria back to Cardiff. The other passengers were silent but friendly. The driver smiled at me as he handed me my ticket. 'There you are love.' I almost hugged him. My double seat felt more like a double bed, it was so comfortable, so warm. I dozed off almost immediately, waking occasionally to see my immediate past pass before me – mountains, sheep, mountains, sheep, and lots of running water. By the time we got to Cardiff, the whole wide world was awake. Crowd scenes everywhere.

My flat had a neglected air. I hadn't yet made any effort to make it mine. It showed. I dumped everything in the washing machine, showered, had a big fry-up. I opened the windows. The sun was shining. It felt good.

Monday. Work. As usual, everyone talking at once. The inevitable third degree. 'What was it like?' 'Better than a health farm?' (My alternative choice.) 'Any half-decent blokes?' And my boss: 'Morning, Linda. How was your retreat?' Everyone was looking at me, listening, waiting. 'Brilliant,' I said, 'bloody brilliant.' And I meant it.

PASSION FRUIT

~

Lindsay Ashford

The bus station in this tatty suburb of Kigali is a hall of mirrors. As I walk towards the street everything I see bulges. The dusty, ramshackle vehicles, the parched potted shrubs and the careworn faces of the travellers are all distorted by the film of tears in my eyes. I blink, searching my bag for something to dab them with, and pull out a paper napkin stamped with the blue logo of Sabena Airlines. I didn't need it on the plane and I don't remember taking it, but there it lies, along with the plastic cutlery and the sachets of salt, pepper and sugar. The stewardess must have thought me very strange, taking the cutlery and leaving the food.

Someone was whispering to me on the plane. An insistent hiss that cut through the hum of the engines and the babble of the other passengers. *You shouldn't be going, you know. This is all wrong. You shouldn't be doing this . . .* I told myself it couldn't be Paul, but it sounded just like him. I wanted to look round, to stand up and shout for help. But I fixed my eyes on the seatback in front of me, counting the little blue squiggles on the grey background until everything began to blur and the whispering slowly died away. No, it couldn't have been his voice. He would have wanted me to come back and find him . . . wouldn't he?

Too late now, anyway. I'm here. I'm back.

I stand at the corner of the street trying to get my bearings. I used to walk along here two, three times a week. Six years on and it is almost unrecognisable. A mangy-looking dog

ambles across and starts sniffing at my feet. As I shoo it away
I catch sight of a stubble of wooden crosses on a patch of bare
earth and my body stiffens. That's the place. The spot where
the school used to be.

I need to go there, touch the ground, feel for his presence,
but my feet are taking me in the opposite direction. Past the
straggling roadside stalls that have sprung up outside the
burnt-out supermarket. As I stumble along a skinny brown
hand holds something out to me. I turn to see a face that is
all teeth. New tears are stretching the woman's features into
a grotesque mask, but as I blink them away I see that she is
really quite beautiful.

Her body is swathed in a brightly patterned cloth of red
and purple and in her outstretched hand is a passion fruit,
cut in half. The juicy, yellow-green flesh makes me realise
that my mouth is bone dry. Seeing me hesitate she stoops
down, pushing a bundle of rags towards me.

'Sit, please,' she says in French.

I sink gratefully onto the makeshift cushion and take the
fruit from her hand. A small head appears from behind the
woman's hips. A child of about four or five years old smiles
shyly at me. He is eating the same fruit as me, the juice
making dark rivulets in the dusty skin of his chin and chest.

'You have come back?' She is looking at me as if she
knows me. Was she one of my patients? I search my memory
for her face, but so many of its images are lost to me now. I
have allowed an impenetrable jungle to spring up around
the Rwanda that I used to know.

'I . . . er . . . I am looking for a friend.' I struggle with my
rusty French. 'He worked at the school.' I nod towards the
patch of crosses.

She nods back slowly, saying nothing. The small boy
wipes his mouth on a fold of her dress but she doesn't seem

to notice. She offers me more fruit and I take it with the ghost of a smile.

The juice is sharp on my tongue. In the old days I would have sprinkled it with sugar or dipped it in a saucerful of rum. I think of the airline sachets in my bag. But no. Sharp is what I need. Something to jar my numbed senses. I bite into the fruit and roll the black seeds around my teeth. Paul's face fills my mind. He used to laugh at my attempts to scoop out the little passion fruit seeds, reminding me that they were edible and telling me not to be so fussy. Now they are gone in one quick swallow.

I open my mouth and words begin to trickle out. To my surprise I find myself telling this woman, this street vendor who I am not sure I have ever met, all about Paul. Well, not quite all. Not about the way he died. She will have guessed that already.

I glance at her face. Hard to estimate her age. Looks mid-twenties but could be late teens. Probably younger rather than older, I decide. Most Rwandan women have four or five children by the time they are twenty-five. I look at the little boy, who ducks behind his mother as my eyes meet his. Is he her first or the youngest of a clutch who are old enough to look after themselves? Whatever, this boy was born after the genocide, so she must have a partner who survived. Who did she lose, then? A father? Brothers? Uncles? The look in her eyes when I pointed to those crosses makes me certain she lost someone. Is that why I am telling her about Paul?

I stop talking and scoop up a bundle of fruit. Perhaps she does this sort of thing all the time. Spotting foreigners whose pain is written on their faces as clearly as the luggage labels on their bags. Peddling her fruit and sympathy in exchange for their precious dollars. Reaching into my bag I pull out a note but when she sees what I am doing she waves it away.

'No, please,' she says, 'you are welcome.'

How cynical I have become. I sometimes feel there is a stone where my heart used to be.

'You made me better,' she adds, mirroring her child's shy smile. 'I had malaria. I came to the hospital . . .'

'Oh, yes,' I lie, 'I think I remember.' How I wish I did. I used to pride myself on never forgetting a patient's face.

A friend back home in Wales persuaded me to go to a therapist. During the first session I was asked to describe the day Paul and I met. But as I summoned up memories of the school, the children waiting in line to be innoculated, Paul holding the hand of each one as the needle went in, I went into hysterics. Ran screaming from the room. I wouldn't, won't go back. I suppose returning to Rwanda is my own, cack-handed attempt at therapy.

I look at the woman again. I am sure she could tell me. She must know about what happened at the school. She must know who lies beneath that grove of crosses. They wouldn't let me anywhere near the place when news of the massacre reached us. I never saw his body, never got the chance to grieve. I open my mouth and close it again. The woman cuts another passion fruit in half and offers it to me. When I shake my head she passes it to her son. How lucky she is to have a child.

I remember hugging myself in misery on the plane out of Kigali, hoping against hope that I might be carrying Paul's child, taking something of him with me. Whisked away by the embassy at the height of the killing, I was back in Wales within a week of his death, treating holidaymakers with sunburn in a surgery in Rhyl. And another week later my period came.

'He was handsome, your friend?' The woman's voice cuts across my thoughts and my mouth tightens.

'Oh yes,' I say. The child flashes me a grin and I do my best to grin back. What would our child have looked like, Paul's and mine? I think about it often. Too often.

'My husband, he was handsome.'

She used the past tense. Is he dead, too? Or is she getting her French grammar muddled? I don't know what to say and to mask my confusion I gesture towards the little boy.

'Yes,' I nod my head, 'Your child is very beautiful.'

'Oh,' she lowers her eyes and strokes the boy's hair, 'He is not my husband's child.' She hesitates a split second. 'His father is a Hutu.'

An atomic flash of horror lights up the images that come crashing through the tangled branches of my memory. Gangs of machete-wielding monsters, their eyes wild with blood-lust. For years I have tried to smother them, to blot them out. But this woman has set them loose. In the aftershock of her words I am only dimly aware of the sounds around me. The buses, the dogs, the people. All are drowned out by the screaming inside my head.

Hutu. Mass-murderers. Paul's murderers.

She raises her eyes from her son's head and looks me full in the face. Her expression has taken on a mask-like quality. Not the distorted death's head I beheld through my tears but a serene countenance fashioned out of pain.

'After they had been to the school they came to my village,' she says. 'They killed my husband in front of me.' She takes a breath. 'They killed my two children.' Another, deeper breath. 'And then,' her hands slip down to cover her child's ears, 'they raped me.'

I stare wordlessly back at her, my mouth falling open. Eventually my voice struggles out in a croak.

'What . . .' I falter, 'What did you do?'

'The nuns took me in.' Her voice sinks to a whisper as the

boy shrugs her hands from his ears. 'He was born in the convent.' She nods her head sideways, indicating the opposite end of the road from the bus station.

'There are many others like me.' Her lips pull in like a drawstring purse. She is fighting to stay in control.

I stare in bewilderment at the child, who has wound his arms around her waist, burying his face in the folds of her dress. Suddenly his head whips round, grins at me, and whips back again. He is playing peek-a-boo. I blink and bite my lip.

'Yes, I do love him,' she says, reading my thoughts. 'For a long, long time I wanted to die. But now he is everything to me.' She bends her head, nuzzling his hair and he laughs. When she looks up there are traces of tears in her eyes. 'I love him . . . too much.'

The sun is sinking low over the bus station when I leave the woman and her son. In my hand I have a passion fruit, cut in half. The patch of earth, reddened by the dying light, feels warm as I stoop to touch it. The powdery soil is easy to scoop out with the plastic airline spoon. Easier than I thought it would be. I pour water from an *Evian* bottle into the hole and place the two halves of fruit side by side. Paul's words float into my mind.

Just try swallowing the seeds. They are edible, you know. They might not look very nice but you'll take forever if you try to pick them out . . .

STRAWBERRY CREAM

~

Siân James

I was eleven that summer, but according to my mother, already moody as a teenager, 'What can I do?' my constant cry. 'I'm bored. What can I do?'

'There's plenty to do. What about dusting the front room for me? Your grandmother and your Auntie Alice are coming to tea on Sunday.'

I hated our front room which was cold and shabby, the furniture old-fashioned, the ceiling flaking and pock-marked with damp and the once mauve and silver wallpaper faded to a sour grey and wrinkled at the corners. Our whole house was depressing, each room having its own distinctive and unpleasant smell, the front room smelling of mushrooms, the living room of yesterday's meat and gravy and the back kitchen of Oxydol and wet washing. 'Dusting doesn't alter anything,' I said.

I expected my mother to argue with me, but she seemed too dispirited. 'I know it doesn't,' she said. And then, 'Just get yourself a nice library book and pretend you live in a palace.'

Was that what she did? She was always reading; two and sixpenny paperback romances with fair-haired girls standing on windy hills on the covers, their skirts gusting out prettily around them, their long tresses streaming behind, but their make-up immaculate.

Once I'd tried reading one of them. *Caterina breathed in as Milly tugged at the corset strings around her waist. 'Tighter,' she commanded sharply.*

'Yes, Miss Caterina,' Milly murmured in a humble voice. She loved her mistress with a blind adoration and wanted nothing but to serve her.

I continued the story in my own way. *Milly squeezed the juice of the deadly nightshade into her mistress's drinking chocolate and chuckled as she imagined pulling the strings of the shroud tighter and tighter around the tiny waist.*

I was fiercely egalitarian. My dad was a farm labourer and he had the same attitude, speaking to his boss with unconcealed disdain. 'You want me to do . . . what?' 'Don't you think that would work?' his boss would ask. 'Of course it wouldn't bloody work, but I'll do whatever you tell me. It's all one to me.'

My mother served in the village shop for two pounds ten a week and she was pretty cool too. I don't think she ever demanded a decent wage, just helped herself to groceries to make up the deficiency, mostly items that fitted neatly into her overall pockets. We were never short of packets of jelly, corn-flour, mixed herbs, caraway seeds. Or bars of chocolate. That summer, Cadbury's Strawberry Cream was my passion and she brought me one every single lunch time. And every afternoon I'd snap the bar into eight squares, sniff every one, bite a hole in the corner and very slowly suck out the oozy pink cream, afterwards letting the sweet chocolate casing melt on my tongue. Sometimes I could make it last a blissful half hour.

My father's boss, Henry Groves, had a daughter called Amanda who was three or four years older than me and went to a boarding school in Malvern. I'm sure she wouldn't have chosen to spend any time with me had there been any older and more sophisticated girls in the village, but there weren't. She'd knock on our front door and stand there silently until I condescended to go out with her.

We usually walked along by the river, kicking at stones and muttering to one another. 'What's your school like?' 'Deadly. What about yours?' 'Deadly.' We had nothing to talk about.

We could never think of anything to do either. What was there to do? The sun beat down on us mercilessly every afternoon, the hours stretched out long and stagnant as sermons; I felt dusty and dried-up as the yellowing grass on the verge of the path.

'Don't you have any adventures at your school?' I asked her one day. 'Don't you have midnight feasts and so on? Pillow-fights in the dorm?' I wanted some sort of conversation; lies would be fine by me. Her eyes narrowed. 'What rubbish have you been reading? How old are you anyway?'

'Thirteen.' She looked across at me. I was tall and sturdy for eleven. She was small and, I suppose, rather pretty; a turned-up nose, floppy hair and so on. My God, she looked a bit like the lovesick girls on the covers of my mother's Mills and Boon. Why was I wasting my summer afternoons with her?

'Well act your age then. Pillow-fights! For God's sake!'

I tried again. 'Do you have a boyfriend?' I asked.

She gave me a friendlier look. 'That would be telling.' I was definitely on the right track.

'I'll tell you if you tell me,' I said, trying to recall conversations I'd overheard on the school bus; a fierce, fat girl called Natalie Fisher, who was about fifteen I suppose, but looked thirty, who was always whispering loudly about 'doing it'. I could pretend I was 'doing it' with Joe Blackwell who sometimes helped me with my Science homework.

'You go first,' she said.

'I've got this boyfriend called Joe Blackwell.'

'And?'

'He's tall and he's got red hair and millions of freckles. Quite attractive.'

'And?'

'And . . . and we "do it" sometimes.'

She was suddenly looking at me with alarming admiration; her eyes dilated and her lips moist. 'Go on,' she said.

'Nothing much more to say. Your turn now.'

'Let's cross the river. It's more private in the woods. We can talk better over the other side.'

We hadn't seen a soul all afternoon, but if she wanted to cross the river I was quite prepared to wade across with her. It made a change.

We took off our sandals and splashed across. The sky was white and glaring, the stones in the riverbed were hot and sharp.

'These are my father's woods,' she said.

There was no answer to that. I knew as well as she did whose bloody woods they were. 'This is where Joe Blackwell and I . . . you know.' I said. It seemed a way to get even with her.

'Show me what you do,' she said, moistening her lips again with the tip of her small pink tongue. 'Show me how you do it.' She sat on the ground and pulled me down with her.

'I can't do it with a girl,' I said, my voice gritty with embarrassment.

'Yes you can, of course you can. Don't you think I know anything.' She was opening her dress and pulling me to her. 'Do you like my breasts?' she asked, tilting them up towards me.

I hated breasts. My Auntie Alice was always getting hers out to feed her baby, great mottled things, large as swedes, but more wobbly. I hated having to see them, the shiny mauve veins; the pale, wet, puckered nipples.

Amanda's breasts were different, small and delicate, creamy as honeysuckle, pink-tipped. She snatched at my hand and placed it over one of them. It seemed like some small, warm animal under the curve of my palm. 'What now?' she asked. 'What do we do next?' Her voice was creaky like the hinge of a gate.

Her nipple hardened under my touch. I felt little shivers go down my body like vibrations in the telegraph wires. I closed my eyes as my fingers circled over and over her breasts. 'We have to do this part properly first,' I said.

I peeped at her face. Her eyes were closed. She looked like the picture of Saint Winifred in church; as though she was seeing angels.

'Now what?' she asked again. I lowered myself onto my elbow and licked her nipples, one after the other. Her eyes flicked open in surprise.

'Licking?' she asked.

'Licking,' I said firmly. 'Don't you like it?'

'I think so. Do you?'

The shivering started up again, it was lower now, my belly seemed fluttery as a nest of fledglings. 'Yes, I like it.' I tried to sound non-committal, but suddenly I was lifting her towards me and sucking, sucking her little round breasts.

'That's all I know,' I confessed at last. Other images which were beginning to besiege my mind seemed altogether too bizarre. 'I don't know the rest of it,' I repeated.

I thought she'd be annoyed, expected her to fasten up her dress and flounce off. She wasn't, though, and didn't. 'Well, we can do this part again, can't we?'

And we did. We did it again and again all through the last dog days of that summer. Every fine afternoon we'd set off wordlessly along the same path, crossing the river at the same spot, lying down under the same trees, finding the same stirrings of pleasure.

At the beginning of September, it got damp and cold, the leaves lost their lustre, the birds grew silent, the woods began to smell of rust and wet earth and we realised that our time was running out.

'I'm going back to school next week,' Amanda said one Friday afternoon, 'so I suppose we'd better say goodbye.'

I raised my mouth from her breast and sat up. 'Goodbye,' I said. I felt something almost like sadness, but wasn't going to let her know it.

'Perhaps we'll do the other part next year,' she said.

'Perhaps.'

I never saw her again. Before the Christmas holidays my father had found a better job and we'd moved from our horrid old house to another that wasn't quite as horrid, and my mother worked in an office instead of a village shop.

I went to a different school and forgot Joe Blackwell. But I never quite forgot those afternoons with Amanda: my strawberry cream summer.

BIOGRAPHICAL NOTES

LINDSAY ASHFORD worked for the BBC as a journalist in the 1980s and then spent ten years freelancing for newspapers and magazines. She moved to Aberystwyth in 1997 where she now works as a reporter for *The Cambrian News*. 'Passion Fruit' is the second short story she has had published. She has also written two crime novels, which are currently with an agent.

GILLIAN BRIGHTMORE was born and educated in Wales. She has published both poetry and short stories. In 1999 she was awarded a Welsh Arts Council Award to work on a collection of short stories. She is at present completing an MA in Scriptwriting at the University of Glamorgan and working on a thriller set in Cardiff and Cardigan.

PATRICIA DUNCKER is Reader in English at the University of Wales, Aberystwyth, where she teaches writing, and nineteenth and twentieth-century literature. She is the author of *Hallucinating Foucault* (1996), *Monsieur Shoushana's Lemon Trees* (1997), and *James Miranda Barry* (1999). A psychological horror novel, *The Deadly Space Between* (Picador, 2002) and a collection of essays, *Writing on the Wall* (Rivers Oram Press), will be published in 2002.

JULIA GREGSON has lived in Wales for twenty years, but began her writing life as a journalist in Australia, and later as a foreign correspondent in New York and Los Angeles, where her articles appeared in the Australian press as well as in the *New York Times*, *Rolling Stone* and *Redbook*. Her first published short story won the *Literary Review* Prize, and since then her stories have been broadcast on Radio 4, and been published in various anthologies and magazines, such as *The Literary Review*, *Good Housekeeping* and *Redbook*. She is currently completing a historical novel set in Wales, and loosely based on Jane Evans, a Welsh woman who ran away with the drovers to join Florence Nightingale in Scutari.

CHRISTINE HARRISON is a novelist and an award winning short story writer. She has been published by Macmillan, Serpents Tail and Honno, and is currently working on a novel.

IMOGEN RHIA HERRAD was born in 1967. She is German originally but lived in Aberystwyth, and has since got a thing about Welsh culture and language. She now lives in London, where she works as a freelance radio journalist, specialising in travel writing and cultural history with a particular interest in women's history and Welsh history, myth and literature. In between she also works as a translator and temp to make ends meet. 'Bronwerdd' is her first published story.

CHLOE HEUCH is a twenty-seven year old English teacher at present living in a small village near Glossop, Derbyshire. She was born in Taunton and is of Welsh/Danish/Yorkshire parentage, and has lived on the Llŷn Peninsula. She has completed an MA in creative writing at Lancaster University and has had numerous poems published in small press publications. Her first short story, 'Seeing Things' was published by Honno in *Catwomen from Hell* (2000). She has also had two poems published in *Blodeuwedd: An Anthology of Women's Poetry* (Headland).

LIZ HINDS was born in Mumbles and has never quite got out of the habit. At sixteen, forced to choose her future, she opted for science. A quarter of a lifetime later, she realised her mistake. Now she dreams and walks and writes and dreams some more, remembering that dreams do sometimes come true, even if, like seeing Paul McCartney, it takes 28 years. Her first short story to be published was 'Bunkered', which was included in *Mama's Baby, Papa's Maybe* (Parthian 1999). She has also been published by *Cambrensis*.

CHRISTINE HIRST was born in Birmingham but now lives in North Wales. Her family, originally from South Wales, lived in the Mountain Ash area. As a young woman she worked as a book reviewer and freelance journalist in Liverpool and later in Connah's Quay, North Wales. After moving to Shropshire she became a teacher and then head-teacher before finally retiring to North Wales. She has been published by Honno and Cambrensis and her work has been shortlisted for the Asham Award. She is currently working on a novel about Welsh convict women in Australia.

JANET HOLCROFT was born in Lancashire but graduated from the University of Wales, Cardiff, in 1976. She remained in Wales and now lives in the Brecon Beacons. She is a full-time teacher who began writing in 2000 and 'The Sugar Pig' is her first published work. At present she is working on a novel, an historical fantasy for children.

GAIL HUGHES was born in Calgary in 1944, of a Welsh father and Canadian mother. She graduated in literature from Edmonton and McGill Universities and then travelled widely in the Middle East, teaching English and working as a jour-nalist and photographer in Dubai, Yemen, Afghanistan and Iran. She settled in Gwynedd in 1983, where she taught lit-erature at the University of Wales and devoted herself to writing and bringing up her three children. She became a director at Tŷ Newydd Writers' Centre in 1996. Several of her short stories were broadcast on BBC Radio 4, and *Flamingos*, her first collection, was published shortly before she died. At the time of her death, in February 2001, Gail was working on a historical novel set in Wales. A gifted linguist, she spoke Arabic, Persian, French and Welsh.

JO MAZELIS (née HUGHES) was born and brought up in Swansea, and has also lived in London and Aberystwyth. She is a photographer and designer and has an MA in Literature from Swansea University. Her stories have appeared in a number of magazines and anthologies, and have also been broadcast on Radio Four. She was one of the winners of the Rhys Davies Short Story Competition in 1995, 1999 and 2001, and was shortlisted for the Asham Award. She lives in Swansea and is currently working on her first novel.

SIÂN JAMES has written eleven novels, with the latest, *Second Chance* appearing in 2000. Her third novel, *A Small Country* (Collins, 1979) was reissued in the Seren Classics series. Her collection of short stories, *Not Singing Exactly* (Honno, 1996) won the Arts Council of Wales Book of the Year Award. Her autobiographical vignettes of a Cardiganshire childhood in the 1930s, *The Sky Over Wales*, was published in 1998 by Honno.

SUSAN MORGAN lives in Cardiff. She has had short stories published by Honno and broadcast on Radio 4. With the help of a Welsh Arts Council bursary she is completing a collection of short stories one of which she adapted for a short film. She must write that novel.

ANN MORUS was born in Sussex and gained a first class Honours B.A. in English and (much later) an M.A. in Modern

English Language, both from the University of London. After teaching English and lecturing in English Language and Linguistics in Baghdad, Lisbon and London she moved to Aberystwyth to work as a freelance writer and editor. As Gwyneth Tyson Roberts she is the author of a linguistic analysis of the 1847 Report on Education in Wales, *The Language of the Blue Books* (University of Wales Press, 1988). Her short stories have appeared in *Fingerprints: Crime Shorts* (1992), *Cambrensis* and *Catwomen From Hell* (Honno, 2000).

MELANIE NEWMAN was brought up in Pembroke and graduated with a degree in biology from Durham University in 1994. After completing a MSc at Essex University she was unable to find a job so retrained as a solicitor. She found a job with a London law firm but left after six months to become a legal journalist. 'Pink Cake' is her first published short story although another of her stories was highly commended in the 1999 Ian St James Awards.

LYNNE REES was born and brought up in Port Talbot, South Wales. After working for seven years in the Channel Islands she moved to Kent in 1985 where she ran her own second-hand/antiquarian bookshop until 1999. She is a graduate of the University of Glamorgan's Masters programme and her poetry has been published by many of the literary journals and anthologised in *Teaching a Chicken to Swim – New Writing from Glamorgan* (Seren 2000). She is currently a tutor in creative writing for the University of Kent at Canterbury.

ANGELA RIGBY was born in Kent and has lived in Wales for twenty-six years. After obtaining a Diploma in Public and Social Administration at Oxford she worked for a voluntary Children's Society and then for a local authority in an experimental project in residential child care. She now lives in Cardiff. Her work has been published in *Social Work Today*, *Cambrensis*, *the New Welsh Review*, the *South Wales Golfer*, the *Collins Anthology of New Christian Verse* (1990) and the *York Poetry Society* magazine.

JENNY SULLIVAN was born in Cardiff too many years ago, but now lives at Raglan. Having left school at 15 she returned to education in 1993 and graduated with an MA in Creative Writing from the University of Wales, Cardiff. She has concluded work for a PhD, also at Cardiff. She has written seven novels for children: the *The Magic Apostrophe* trilogy, *The Back End of Nowhere, Following Blue Water, Gwydion and the Flying Wand,* and *Who, me?*, the first part of a second trilogy in the Magic Apostrophe series. The second part of the *Gwydion . . .* trilogy *Magic Meldwyn* will be published in 2002. In addition she has written *Sion and the Bargain Bee* and *Two Left Feet*, both picture books, and a third, *The Caterpillar that Couldn't*, is due for publication in Spring 2002. Jenny also writes short stories and poetry for both adults and children – when she isn't visiting schools all over Wales for workshops – and fun.

JANET THOMAS was born and brought up in Aberystwyth. After living in London for several years, through college and then as a secretary, editorial assistant and editor at Hodder & Stoughton Children's Books, she returned to Aberystwyth, where she works as a freelance editor. She had a story published in *Power* (Honno) and edited *Catwomen from Hell* (Honno).

SARAH TODD was born in Lancashire and graduated from UWA Aberystwyth in 1998 with a PhD in History. Her essay on the presentation of violent women in seventeenth-century balladry was published in *Women's History Notebooks* in 1994, but 'Last Night's Dinner' is her first piece of published fiction.

ALEXANDRA WARD is a South Walian presently living in Norfolk. Her serious education began in the late sixties when she became a student at Coleg Harlech. From there she went on to University College, Cardiff, and did research at the University of East Anglia. Her short stories have appeared in Honno's previous anthologies *Luminous and Forlorn, Power,* and *Catwomen from Hell,* and in *The New Welsh Review.* She is a descendant of Lucy Thomas, Abercanaid, a pioneer of the Welsh coal industry.

NIA WILLIAMS was born in Cardiff in 1961 and studied History at Exeter University and European Studies at Reading. Her short stories have appeared in *Cambrensis* magazine and in the anthologies *Power* and *Catwomen from Hell* (Honno), *Tilting at Windmills* and *Mama's Baby (Papa's Maybe)* (Parthian), and have been broadcast on Radio Wales and Radio 4. Her highly-commended first novel *The Pier Glass* was published by Honno in 2001. She lives in Oxford, where she works as a freelance writer and editor.

PENNY ANNE WINDSOR is a Cornishwoman who has lived in Wales for many years. She teaches creative writing and literature to a wide variety of adult education groups and is presently studying for a M.A. in Education (Lifelong Learning) with the Open University. She is widely published as a poet and short story writer, including two collections of poems published by Honno. She has stories published in *The New Penguin Book of Welsh Short Stories, Luminous and Forlorn* (Honno), *Mamma's Baby (Pappa's Maybe)* (Parthian), *Cambrensis* etc., and broadcast on BBC Radio 4. She has recently completed a collection of her poetry for schoolchildren, *A Cut Above the Usual,* as a result of receiving the Irma Chilton Award for Children's Writing in 2000.

ABOUT HONNO

Honno Welsh Women's Press was set up in 1986 by a group of women who felt strongly that women in Wales needed wider opportunities to see their writing in print and to become involved in the publishing process. Our aim is to publish books by, and for, women of Wales, and our brief encompasses fiction, poetry, children's books, autobiograpical writing and reprints of classic titles in English and Welsh.

Honno is registered as a community co-operative and so far we have raised capital by selling shares at £5 a time to over 400 interested women all over the world. Any profit we make goes towards the cost of future publications. We hope that many more women will be able to help us in this way. Shareholders' liability is limited to the amount invested, and each shareholder, regardless of the number of shares held, will have her say in the company and a vote at the AGM. To buy shares, to buy books directly, to be added to our database of authors or to receive further information about forthcoming publications, please e-mail:

information@honno.co.uk or write to Honno:
'Ailsa Craig',
Heol y Cawl, Dinas Powys,
Bro Morgannwg CF64 4AH.

www.honno.co.uk

ALSO AVAILABLE
FROM HONNO:

*A View across the Valley:
Short Stories by Women from Wales 1850-1950*
Edited by Jane Aaron

Stories by
Allen Raine, Dorothy Edwards, Hilda Vaughan,
Brenda Chamberlain, Margiad Evans and others

This rich and diverse collection of twenty short stories
provides an opportunity for the modern reader to discover
a lost tradition of English-language storytelling by women
from Wales, as most of the stories have never been re-
published since their first appearance in print. As well as
being entertaining – and often moving – in themselves,
the stories demonstrate how late nineteenth and early
twentieth-century women contributed to the development
of Welsh culture and identity, although their contribution
has since been forgotten.

The volume also includes a general introduction, and
biographical and textual notes on each author and text.
Jane Aaron is a Professor of English at the University of
Glamorgan, and is a renowned expert on Welsh women's
writing.

£7.95   ISBN 1 870206 35 5

Power
An Anthology of Short Stories by Women from Wales
Edited by Elin ap Hywel

Some women learn about power young. Take Emma –
though she's only a child, she can tell what the grown-ups
are saying through walls and locked doors.

Some women, on the other hand, keep their power hidden
inside them for years. Like Mary-Jayne Evans; though she's
dead, her body's as lovely as ever. Or Mrs Scarlatti, who's
very much alive. Or Penny, or Lily, or Meinir or Gail . . .

Honno's second collection of short stories by women from
Wales looks at where power lives – and where it lies
concealed – in women's lives. Jo Hughes, Clare Morgan,
Nia Williams and Jenny Sullivan are among the authors
who reveal that our powers are often more surprising –
and more potent – than meet the eye.

£7.95   ISBN 1 870206 26 6